The Colored Car

GREAT LAKES BOOKS

*A complete listing of the books in this series
can be found online at wsupress.wayne.edu*

The Colored Car
Jean Alicia Elster

 Wayne State University Press / Detroit

17 16 15 14 13   5 4 3 2 1

ISBN 978-0-8143-3606-9 (paperback)
ISBN 978-0-8143-3608-3 (e-book)

Library of Congress Control Number: 2013941837

♾

Designed and typeset by Maya Whelan
Composed in Century Old Style Std and Clarendon MT

In loving memory of my cousin, *Billy,*
this book is dedicated to *Gwynn,* my sister and friend,
and to my Ford cousins—

Debbie

Dwight

Darryl

Merle

M.T.

Herbie

Nancy

Michael

Cheryl

Mark

and

Mel

Contents

Acknowledgments

I offer my utmost gratitude to my mother, Jean Ford Fuqua, and my aunt, Maber Ford Hill, for their willingness to share more tales from their youth.

All due appreciation to my editor, Kathryn Wildfong, for opening the door to this second volume in the Ford family story. (Kathy, you're the best.)

Deepest thanks to my son, Isaac Elster, for giving each chapter a first read and for sharing his gut reactions with me.

Also thanks to my dear friend, Debra Darvick, for guiding me to the "real story." Grateful acknowledgment to my friend and fellow wordsmith Sharon Gordon, for helping me see that my best thoughts come in the morning. Special regards to Professor Nichelle Boyd and her "Ole Miss" 2011 fall term Social Studies Methods students for enthusiastically sharing a bit of Southern culture with me.

Acknowledgments

As always, I offer my heartfelt gratitude to my husband, Bill, for filling this writer's life with love and joy.

Prologue

The history of the struggle for civil rights in the United States—the attempt by African Americans to possess basic rights of American citizenship that were denied to them based upon racial discrimination—can be studied through the progression of lawsuits filed by black passengers challenging segregation, or the separation of blacks and whites, on the nation's railroads, particularly when traveling in the South.

As more railroad tracks were laid across the country during the 1860s, the importance of train travel grew. So much so that by the late 1800s, trains became the primary mode of long-distance travel in the United States until the mid-1950s, when cars, buses, and airplanes grew in popularity. It was after 1865—following the end of the Civil War and during the time known as Reconstruction—that African Americans sought to enjoy equal rights as citizens not just in the states and towns where they lived but also when traveling throughout the country.

During the nineteenth and much of the twentieth centuries, black Americans were generally referred to as "colored." When traveling in the North, "colored" passengers could sit according to the class or type of ticket they purchased. The problem came when traveling in the South. Black and white travelers could not sit in the same train cars. And if a train ride started in a northern state, when the train entered a southern state—or crossed what was called the Mason-Dixon Line—black riders were made to leave their seats and sit in an all-black or "colored" train car.

Over the years, a large number of lawsuits were filed by African American passengers who had been forced—often dragged—from their seats and into segregated cars when traveling on southern rail lines. However, the law of the land was established by the 1896 U.S. Supreme Court case *Plessy v. Ferguson*. That case held that states had the right to require "separate but equal" seating for black passengers. This segregation was enforced by what were known as "Jim Crow" laws in the South and extended far beyond separate seating on train cars. Legalized segregation applied to all manner of public facilities including theaters, restrooms, public transportation, and water fountains. However, in northern cities, segregation was not enforced by law. Rather, it existed in practice and tradition, with the end result often manifesting itself not so much in public facilities but in primarily segregated neighborhoods, schools, and churches.

The effects of the court decision in *Plessy v. Ferguson* and the notion of "separate but equal" were far-reaching, leaving very few aspects of American public life untouched. It remained the law in the United States for decades to come.

Piccalilli

Mounds of ground-up onions, celery, cabbage, and sweet green peppers were piled high on the table in the middle of the summer kitchen—Patsy did not have to ask her mother what she was making. In the early weeks in July, it was the first recipe May Ford put up in jars each year. "Piccalilli," it was called. Some of the neighbor women, the ones from the South, called it "cha-cha." Patsy stood by the table and watched her mother push heaps of those vegetables through the mouth of the grinder, sometimes leaning in hard as she turned the crank.

Patsy's three younger sisters were napping over in the back room. Before this summer, she would have lain down next to them and dozed off, too. But since her brother, Doug Jr., was working with their father in his wood business and riding in the truck, she had been given one of his chores. Doug, the oldest, was fourteen years old now. She was twelve. "Old enough," her mother had told her. Throughout the day, it was now Patsy's job to fill bucket after bucket of water from the faucet located off the back porch of the house just as she had seen her brother do so many times before. Now she was the one who would lug them into the summer kitchen for her mother to use as she cooked. There would be no time for her to take a nap.

"Patsy," May Ford said as she looked over her shoulder at her daughter. Then she motioned with her head to a row of empty buckets under the table where she worked. "Don't let all of the buckets get empty like that. Get going, honey."

"Yes, Mama," Patsy said. She quickly reached under the table and grabbed one of the pails. She headed outside to the faucet, filling the bucket to the brim and sloshing water along the driveway as she returned to the summer kitchen. She could hear their old hound dog, Pointo, noisily lapping up the puddles of water. She filled all the empty buckets.

The pungent smell of onions was heavy in the air, and tears—caused by the juice of the onions as she fed them into the grinder—streamed down May's face. Patsy quickly stepped back as she placed the final bucket under the table. Her eyes burned, too, and teared up from the onions. She stood at the doorway next to the long wooden bench against the wall and rubbed her eyes, barely able to see the onions ooze out of the grinder all crushed and minced. Straight across the room against the other sidewall, on top of the wide wood-burning cooking stove, a large pot held what smelled to Patsy like boiling vinegar. She knew her mother would, later, mix together all of the crushed-up vegetables and, after filling rows of jars with the mixture, pour hot, spicy vinegar into each one, filling them almost to the rim.

Of all the foods her mother canned each summer, piccalilli was Patsy's favorite because the taste was so different: it was sweet and sour, hot and mild. Patsy liked it most when her mother stirred it in with potato salads, spread it across slices of bread for ham sandwiches, and sometimes scooped it next to fried eggs for Sunday breakfasts. It was—

"Mama, I'm hot!" It was Patsy's baby sister Annie May, calling from the back room.

There was a small room adjacent to the summer kitchen. It was first built as a storage area for May Ford's jars of canned fruits and vegetables. While cabinets were still lined up along the walls, there was now a brass bed right in the middle of the room, where the Ford sisters sat and played with their dolls, or made up hand-to-hand clapping chants and string games, and took their naps. Patsy had heard the story, many times, of how her father, Douglas Ford, built the summer kitchen and the adjoining storage room for his young wife. It went up not too long after he had built the family's home on Halleck Street, and shortly after going back south to Clarksville, Tennessee, to marry his bride and bring her up to Detroit in 1922. The summer kitchen was a two-room whitewashed wooden building with a floor made of wide planks of lumber. It stood in the back of the lot across from the house and behind the wood yard that was a part of the Douglas Ford Wood Company. It was where her mother could do all of her canning and not heat up their home. Giving off more heat—in the already hot summer months—was a large wood-burning stove, the first thing anyone laid eyes on when they stepped into the room. Patsy's father filled it with heavy pieces of oak first thing in the morning before he left in his truck and then again in the afternoon when he returned home from his morning runs. The fire never died down during the canning season.

The summer kitchen was where May could be found, especially during the months of July and August, it seemed to Patsy, from sunup to sundown. Her mother did leave the summer kitchen and go into the house to prepare lunch or cook dinner for the family. She sometimes went inside to wash a load of clothes in her wringer washing machine. Or she hurried in when the phone rang to take a customer's order for a cord of wood. But until almost nightfall, everything else pretty much happened in and around the summer kitchen.

"Mama, I'm hot!" Annie May called out again.

Patsy turned and hurried into the back room and scooped her baby sister up off the bed.

"Gotcha!" Patsy said, planting a kiss on her cheek.

"Mama! Annie May wet the bed!" Laura yelled out.

"Yee-uck!" Jean squealed.

"Oh, my," May Ford said, steadily mixing together the ground-up vegetables.

"No, I didn't!" Annie May said.

"Then how come the bed's wet right where you were lying down? Huh?" Laura asked.

"No, I didn't, I didn't!" Annie May insisted. She started to cry.

"You girls . . . Patsy, what's going on in there?" their mother asked, still working at the table.

Patsy put her sister down and leaned over the wet spot in the bed. She sniffed.

"No she didn't, Mama," Patsy said. "She just sweated a lot in her sleep."

"But the bed's wet," Laura said. "Look," she added, pointing at a large spot on the bottom sheet.

"The wet spot doesn't smell like pee," Patsy said, looking directly at Laura. She used her sleeve to wipe more sweat off of Annie's forehead. "The bed just feels wet. But it's just sweat."

"It *is* hot in here," their mother said and wiped

the beads of perspiration off of her nose with the back of her hand. "Patsy, pull open the curtains in here and in the back room. We need to get some breezes blowing in around here. But I tell you, breezes or not—nothing's going to cool off this ole summer kitchen," she said as she pulled her apron up to her forehead and wiped down her entire face. "Putting food up, it's always going to be hot in here . . ."

During the summer months, when fruits and vegetables were ripe and ready, May Ford canned—put up in jars—food for the family to eat for the rest of the year. She stood at the table with her kitchen knives and the grinder and prepared the fruits and vegetables as they came in season. Peaches, pears, cherries, grapes, tomatoes, corn, string beans, okra . . . everything that came in season. She ground, chopped, cored, halved, sliced, peeled, pitted— whatever she needed to do to get the food ready to go in the pot and then into the jars.

Peddlers rode down Halleck Street just to drive past the Ford house during canning season. Most of them came plodding by in horse-drawn carts with Italian names painted on the sides. It was one of the few times the girls saw horses on the streets of Detroit. "Fresh fruits! Fresh fruits and vegetables!" they called out. They knew all about May Ford and what went on in the summer kitchen. The girls could hear them holler as they turned off of Dequindre Road and onto Halleck Street. The house was not far from the corner, and the peddlers kept a slow pace as they approached the house, hoping Douglas Ford would flag them over so that he could look at their produce and they could thank him and promise to have even more of what he wanted the next time they passed through. "Fresh fruits! Get your fruits and vegetables!" He bought bushels at a time as the fruits and vegetables came in season. And the produce had to be just right, perfectly ripe, because, he explained, his wife chopped, ground, boiled—whatever needed to be done— and poured it into jars that very same day.

The girls—Laura, who was ten years old, Jean, who was eight, and Annie May, only three— followed Patsy around the back room and then out into the summer kitchen as she spread open the curtain panels.

"Patsy, now go in the house and make us some lemonade," May said, adding, "Girls, you go with your sister. And Patsy, chip some ice from the icebox. I want the lemonade real cold."

"Should I change the baby's sundress, put a dry one on her?" Patsy asked her mother.

"No—not in this heat. She'll be nice and dry in no time."

"M-m-m-mam-m-m . . ." It was Jean. She tapped her mother's arm. "Mama, c-c-c-c-c . . ." She tensed her body as she tried to get the words out. Her head twitched to the right as she tried to speak.

"She wants to know if she can help, too," Laura interrupted.

"Laura, what have I told you," their mother scolded. "Let her talk. She can speak for herself."

"No she can't," Laura answered and started giggling.

Patsy turned toward Laura and said in a low voice, "Laura, stop it!" Laura looked her in the eyes and stuck out her tongue.

"Jean." Their mother looked away from her work and spoke directly to her daughter,

"Remember—when you can't say one word, just use another."

"C-c-c-c," Jean stopped, her head still. She took a breath. "Let me help, too!"

"Of course, dear, you can help your sister." May turned to Patsy. "Let Jean stir the lemonade."

"Yes, Mama," Patsy answered as she took Annie May's hand.

"I wanna stir, too," Annie May said, pouting.

"Everybody gets to stir," Patsy said, leading her sisters into the yard.

∽

Patsy told the girls to sit under the tree while she carried the pitcher of ice-cold lemonade to their mother. As Patsy walked toward the summer kitchen, she could already smell Mrs. Carson's strong perfume, even over the odor of the onions. So she was not surprised to see her and some of the neighbor women visiting with her mother, standing by her at the table—Mrs. Eva Yablonski from next door, Mrs. Cleota Chambers, their next-door neighbor on the other side, and Mrs. Sadie Carson from across the street. Mrs. Chambers, who was heavyset and who always seemed to be out of breath, was fanning herself with her apron. They were talking, and while Mrs. Yablonski's heavy Polish accent stood out as she talked with the colored neighbors, Patsy could barely make out what any of them were saying, their voices were so low. Patsy heard the words "hungry" and "food" and "drink." It was 1937 and she was used to hearing the women talk about the Depression when they visited and how hard times were for almost everybody. She assumed that's what they were talking about then. The ladies stopped talking altogether when Patsy walked into the room.

"Here's my girl," May Ford announced, briefly looking up from the table. Working as she talked, she scooped up some vegetable mixture with a large spoon and put it in each of a dozen or so quart-sized jars lined up on the table. "Patsy, pour some lemonade in those tin cups for you and your sisters and go cool off out in the yard. There should be some nice shade under the tree," she directed her daughter.

Patsy did just that, gingerly holding the four

cups by their handles, one each for Jean, Laura, Annie May, and herself.

"Now Sadie, please—go get some of those glasses over there on the shelf and pour us some lemonade before the ice melts."

Once outside, from where she and the girls sat under the tree, Patsy could easily see the women talking, but she had to strain to hear their conversation.

"Well, May, you can't feed the whole neighborhood," Mrs. Carson said, holding the cold glass up to her forehead.

"I know, Sadie, but I'm not going to let those children go hungry," May said. "I'm just going to send enough to tide them over. They're just going through a rough spot."

Mrs. Chambers said, "Now, you know it's not just a rough spot." She stopped as if to catch her breath. "That Mr. Williams—"

"Hush, now! I don't want the girls to hear."

"Well, I'm just saying—"

"You hush!"

There was a silence. Patsy could hear ice clinking against the sides of their glasses as the women finished their lemonade.

Mrs. Carson spoke first. "I heard from my people—got a letter this week, in fact—they're still cleaning up from last spring's flood along the Cumberland." She was from Tennessee, like Patsy's mother. Both grew up in Montgomery County along the Cumberland River, but Patsy's mother grew up in Clarksville and Mrs. Carson was from Palmyra. "How're things in Clarksville? Have you heard anything lately?"

"My mother hasn't said anything about the flood in a long time. Right after it happened, she sent me a telegram—*Big flood. Family is fine. Love, Mother*. Then I got a letter a few weeks later. She said they were spared the worst of it," May said, "and I left it at that." She paused and then asked, "Your people are still cleaning up?"

"Yes, yes, but that's Palmyra. Can't say what's what in Clarksville," Mrs. Carson said.

"Maybe I should visit. I haven't been back home since before Jean was born. Laura was just a babe and Patsy was younger than Annie May. Good Lord, it's been ten years since I've been back to Clarksville! My mama's been here to visit a couple of times, but, come to think of it, the last time I went down there it was after the flood. It was after the flood of 1927, I went to check on my Mama back then. You're right, I need to be down there."

"I'm sure she'd let you know if she needed help, if things were really bad. And your sisters are there to help," Mrs. Chambers said, sounding short of breath.

"Cleota, I need to check on things for myself. My sister Addie sent me a clipping from the newspaper a while ago. It said this flood was even worse than the one in '27. . ."

"I didn't mean to scare you," Mrs. Carson said.

"I'm sure they're all right, Mrs. Ford," Mrs. Yablonski interjected. "And you have plenty to do up here putting up your food and taking care of the children."

"No, I have to talk to Douglas about this. Ten years—time gets away from you. The girls will come with me. They're old enough to take that long train ride. I need to see for myself—I need to check on my mama."

⤴

The ladies were long gone. Jean and Vochu,

Mrs. Yablonski's youngest daughter, were standing one on either side of the fence in their own backyards, whispering to each other and playing with their dolls. Laura sat on the back porch steps, braiding Annie May's hair.

"Ouch!" Annie May cried out.

"I'm not hurting you. You're just tender-headed, that's all," Laura said.

Patsy stood in the doorway to the summer kitchen. The vinegar and pickling spices were boiling in a large pot on the stove. The odor of vinegar mixed with cinnamon, ginger, mustard, and cloves wafting up from that pot grew so sharp that the inside of Patsy's nose started to burn. She held her sleeve up to her nostrils until the tingling stopped. May Ford brought the pot of boiling vinegar over to the table.

"Can I help you, Mama?" Patsy asked. She walked over to her mother and watched her carefully dip the ladle into the steaming hot, spicy mixture and pour it into each jar, covering the vegetables but not quite filling the jar to the top. Standing so close to the pot of vinegar made the inside of her nose burn again.

"Patsy," her mother said, still pouring, "I want

you to go look in the cabinets in the back room and bring a jar of peaches. Find a jar of string beans and maybe okra. Bring one of each of those, too."

"Laura," she called out, "come here! I want you to help Patsy."

"But I'm still braiding Annie's hair," she answered.

"Laura!"

Laura ran to her mother. Annie May sat on the porch steps braiding her doll's hair, her own hair still half-finished. Patsy brought the jars into the front room and laid them on the table.

"Laura, take one of the jars. Patsy, you hold the other two. I want you to take them down the street to Mrs. Williams—"

"Ah, Ma—," Laura said.

"Hush now. I want you to take them down and then come right back home. Don't stay to play with the little Williams girls. Laura, don't you stop to play with Dottie Chambers on the way home. Just tell Mrs. Williams that your mother sent her these jars and get right back home, you hear?"

"Yes, Mama," Patsy answered.

"Laura, you understand?" she asked.

"Mmm-hmm."

"Again?"

"Yes, Mama."

"OK, now. And be careful how you walk. I don't want either one of you to trip and fall and break those jars and cut yourselves."

Patsy and Laura walked slowly down the block, holding the jars close to them, careful not to trip or bump into each other. They were greeted by their neighbors as they walked by— immigrants from eastern Europe who spoke with heavy Polish and German accents—and colored neighbors from the South, many of whom still had a slight drawl when they spoke. The girls nodded and answered each one politely yet quickly, careful to watch their step as they returned the greetings.

The sisters knew the house: it was the second house from the corner on that side of the block, and the Williamses were the only colored family on that end of the street. But they did not have to count from the corner that day because they saw Mr. Williams sitting on the front porch and leaning against the railing. He was breathing heavily and there was a funny, sour smell about him. He looked like he was asleep; his eyes were half-open. Patsy and Laura walked around to the backyard, where Mrs. Williams was hanging some sheets on the clothesline. They told her what their mother had said and handed her the jars.

"You tell your mother, thank you kindly," she told the girls.

They hurried out of the backyard and came around the porch. Mr. Williams leaned forward and yelled out, "Lena, we don't need that food. I can feed my family!" Then he fell back against the railing.

Patsy stopped for a second and looked at him. He stared back at her and growled, "You tell your mother, don't send you down here with no more food!"

Patsy grabbed Laura's hand and they ran down the street back home.

౿

Patsy and Laura were out of breath when they reached their house. They rushed up the driveway and into the summer kitchen. May

Ford was twisting tops onto the jars of piccalilli. Jean and Annie May were sitting on the bench to the side of the doorway, playing with a piece of wood from their father's wood yard.

"Mrs. Williams said to thank you for the food," Patsy reported.

"And Mr. Williams said don't send us down there with any more food," Laura added. "And, Mama, he smelled funny, too!"

"Did he now," their mother said, putting tops on the last of the jars. "Thank you, girls."

They stood and watched as she took a pair of large tongs and, one at a time, grabbed a jar, carefully took it over to the stove, and placed it in a pot of boiling water.

"You girls go on in the house and practice your piano lessons. I'll be finishing up now."

As Patsy followed behind her sisters, she glanced down the driveway. Then she stopped walking, turned, and ran back into the summer kitchen. "Ma! Mr. Williams is coming up the driveway and he's walking kinda funny! Like he can barely stand up straight."

"Thank you, dear." Her mother spoke calmly and deliberately. "Now, I want you to go into the house with your sisters." Patsy stood there. "Go on, now!"

Patsy turned and did as she was told.

Pointo, their hound dog, who had been lying near the tree most of the day, started barking.

The girls watched—and listened—through the screen in the open kitchen window. May Ford walked out into the yard, tongs still in her hand.

"Good evening, Mr. Williams," May Ford said politely, as he stopped just outside the doorway of the summer kitchen.

"You got no right to send food down to my wife." He swayed back and forth as he spoke.

"Just being neighborly. I have more than I can use here."

"You're just an ole busybody." He stepped closer to May. She moved back, being careful not to step back into the summer kitchen.

He pointed a finger, just inches from her face. "Just an ole busybody," he repeated.

May held up the tongs in front of her face. Mr. Williams reached for them. She stepped to the side. He lurched forward and fell on his face. She hurried past him and ran up the back steps and into the house, locking the door behind her. She joined the four girls looking out the kitchen window. Pointo—still barking—ran over to where he lay.

"Daddy's comin'!" Laura announced.

"I hear his truck," Patsy confirmed.

Douglas Ford pulled up in the driveway. He jumped out of the cab of his pickup truck. He took long strides over to the summer kitchen. Doug Jr. followed right behind him. Mr. Williams was having trouble picking himself up off the ground.

"May?" Douglas called out.

"Douglas, I'm in the kitchen with the girls," she said through the window.

Doug Jr. shushed the dog. Their father grabbed Mr. Williams by the back of the collar and pulled him up.

"Your wife's an ole busybody. Tell her don't bring no more food down to my house!"

"Harold, and I'm tellin' *you* something." Douglas turned the man around and looked him straight in the eye. "Don't you ever set foot on my property, around my family, again," Douglas Ford said with anger in his voice.

Mr. Williams pulled himself away. He almost fell over once more. "Aargh! Get away from me." He stumbled back down the driveway.

Douglas Ford shook his head and waited until the man was out of sight before going in the house.

"May? Girls? Is everybody all right?" Douglas Ford asked as he entered the kitchen. The girls ran up to him and hugged him.

"Yes, yes we're all fine," May said. She then explained what happened. "Cleota and Sadie told me the Williams kids were hungry. I just sent something down for them—"

"May," Doug interrupted her and gave her a hug, "I know you're trying to do what's right, but you've done all you can do. Let it go, now. Some things you just can't change."

Grandma Ford's Piccalilli

Recipe courtesy of the Ford family archives

6 green tomatoes
6 red and green sweet peppers
6 onions
1 small winter cabbage
¼ cup salt
2 cups vinegar
2 ½ cups brown sugar
2 tablespoons pickling spices
4 hot peppers
2 cups celery
2 cups carrots

1. Chop up vegetables. Sprinkle with salt, cover, and let stand overnight. Drain.
2. Cover with fresh water and drain again.
3. Tie spices in a small cloth bag. Add to vinegar and sugar. Bring to boil.
4. Reduce heat and simmer for ½ hour.
5. Remove spice bag.
6. Put vegetables in hot jars, leaving ½ inch of headroom at top of jar.
7. Fill jars with hot vinegar.
8. Adjust lids and process in boiling water bath for ten minutes.
9. Allow piccalilli to marinate at least six weeks before opening.

The Baker Streetcar

The next morning, the girls were jammed in together between the dresser and the foot of the bed in their parents' bedroom off the dining room. The heavy scent of their mother's perfume—Desert Flowers—hung in the air as Patsy dabbed some behind her sisters' ears. Laura squeezed ahead of Jean, and Annie May poked her head between the two of them.

"You gave Jean more than you gave me!" Laura said, leaning forward. "Put some more on me."

"Me, too," Annie May insisted. "I want to smell, too!"

"I didn't give Jean more than you," Patsy answered, turning to Laura. "You have enough. Now shush before Mama comes in here!"

"Shush nothing," May Ford said, walking into

the bedroom. Patsy quickly hid the bottle of perfume behind her back.

"I know what you're doing." Their mother held out her palm, and Patsy slowly put the bottle in her hand. "I could smell you girls in my perfume when I walked into the dining room," she said, putting the bottle back on the dresser. Then she clapped her hands. "Come on, now. Into the kitchen. Oatmeal's ready."

The girls hurried into the kitchen and sat around the table in their usual places. Their mother lifted Annie May into the high chair, but she was almost too big to fit. "Goodness, girl," the mother said, "I'm going to have to find a place for you around this table." Then she turned to Patsy. "Go call your father and brother in for breakfast."

Douglas Ford and his drivers had brought in an extra-large haul of scrap wood from the auto factories the day before. He had been out in the wood yard late last night cutting the lumber down to size at the big, loud donkey saw, tossing the smaller pieces into the huge pile behind him. Patsy could hear him back at it, Pointo barking with the sound of the saw, even as she woke up that morning. She looked out the kitchen window and did as she was told. She pushed her forehead against the screen as she called out to them. She could see her father at the saw and her brother, Doug, busy filling one of the trucks with armfuls of wood for deliveries later in the day.

"Oatmeal!" she called. Patsy had to call just once. She could tell they heard her as she pulled her head back: first to stop was the *hee-haw* sound from the donkey saw. Then she didn't hear her brother throwing any more wood into the bed of the truck. They were heading in for breakfast.

When they came into the house, Douglas Ford took one look at the table before he sat down and said, "May, I need some milk for my oatmeal."

"Mr. Scott hasn't been by yet," she said, filling her husband's bowl last of all.

Mr. Scott, the milkman, delivered a quart bottle of milk each morning to the Ford home on Halleck Street, leaving it on the back porch. Their house was his only delivery in the neighborhood. He was also a neighbor: he, his wife, and their two boys lived one street north on McLean. Mr. Scott would sometimes come by in the evening if he needed to see if their father happened to have a spare part or a tool he might be able to use when he was working on his truck or just to talk business. In the morning, Patsy listened for the sound of his deep voice calling out, "Miiiiiilk!" He sounded almost like her father. He had dark brown skin like her father, too.

If Patsy didn't hurry to bring in the milk, Laura would beat her to it and most times drink the thick cream that had risen to the top of the bottle before Patsy or her mother had a chance to shake up the milk in the bottle. Laura always said she didn't do it, that the milk came without the cream, but Patsy knew better and rushed to get the milk just the same.

"No matter," their father said, already eating.

"Are you going to the train station to get the tickets today?" May asked him as she sat down close to Annie.

"W-w-w-whe- . . ." Jean started to say.

"Where's Daddy going?" Laura broke in.

"Can we go, too?" Patsy asked.

"May, are you sure you want to go down there? It's hotter 'n blazes down there mid-July." He looked across the table to where his wife sat.

"Yes, I'm sure. Mother says the flood didn't do that much damage to the house, but I just want to go and see for myself. I just want to check in on her. Make sure everything's OK. "

"Your two sisters are down there. They'd let you know if something was wrong," Douglas said.

"I just want to see for myself," she said. "The article in the paper said it was worse than the flood of '27."

"But May," he said, still eating, "what about your canning? You just got started. The fruit and vegetables are starting to come in . . ."

"I think I've put up enough piccalilli for now. And it's another couple of weeks, end of July, before the early grapes and the peaches come in. Now's as good a time as it's gonna get." She was adamant.

"Can we go, too?" Patsy asked, again.

"W-w-w-whe- . . ." Jean still tried to get the word out.

"Clarksville, baby," the mother said to Jean.

"Tennessee. And Annie, stop playing with your oatmeal," she scolded as she caught Annie May, hand in her bowl, squeezing her food between her fingers.

Douglas Ford leaned in over his breakfast now as he spoke. "Who's going to answer the phone? Take the orders?" He paused and shook his head. "I'm gonna lose a lot of business!"

"They'll call back in the evening," May assured him. "You'll get the orders when you're back from your runs. You think I run in here every time that phone rings when I'm out, up to my arms in cabbage and onions?" She didn't wait for an answer. "Anyway, honey, it's summer. Folks aren't heating their homes in the middle of July."

"Folks are placing orders now for winter, you know that."

"Douglas, I've made up my mind. Seems like the only time I get to Clarksville is when there's a flood. Ten years since I've been home!"

"Goodness, May, I need Doug here at home to help me load the truck and make my deliveries . . ."

"OK—then it'll just be me and the girls. Just get five tickets for Clarksville."

Patsy, Laura, and Jean let out a shriek. Annie, startled by the noise, knocked her bowl to the floor and started crying.

"We're going to Tennessee! We're going to Tennessee!" the two oldest girls said over and over. Jean clapped her hands and grinned.

"I wanna go, too!" Annie May said, still crying. "Mama . . ."

Doug, who had been sitting silently up to now, put his elbows on the table and said, "Ma, who's gonna cook? What're we gonna eat while you're gone?"

Their father chuckled. May shushed the girls.

"Doug, I'm surprised at you. You know your Daddy's a good cook," she said as she wiped Annie's oatmeal up off the floor.

"All I've ever seen Daddy cook is gumbo for Sunday dinner. So I guess it'll be gumbo every night," Doug said with a sigh.

"And it's the best gumbo you'll eat this side of New Orleans," their father assured him. He pronounced it, "N'awlins." He was born, raised, and educated down there. He had been a chauffeur and cook before moving up north in 1922. "And I'll have you know, I can make more than just gumbo. Maybe I'll make a big pot of jambalaya."

"Jumbo what?" Doug asked.

"Jambalaya—sausage, chicken, shrimp, cut up some peppers and tomatoes," their father explained.

"Why don't you make some dirty rice to go along with it?" May asked, smiling.

"Ah, Ma, dirty rice . . ." Doug said.

"Eee-yuck!" Patsy, Laura, and Jean said, almost at the same time.

"Did the rice fall on the floor, Daddy?" Annie May asked.

"Oh children, it's not really dirty. It's just white rice with chicken livers and gizzards mixed in with it. Good idea, May," he said with a grin. Then he put down his spoon and looked at his wife. "OK, I'll get five tickets."

"One week. We'll be there and back before you know it," May said, looking at her husband and son. She said to her daughters, "Now girls, line up to get your hair braided. Then out of your pajamas and into your petticoats and dresses—

we're going downtown to do some shopping. I'm going to make each of you a new dress to wear on the train."

༄

The four sisters and their mother waited at the streetcar stop just off the corner of Joseph Campau and Halleck Streets. They were waiting for the Baker streetcar. The Baker car would take them straight down Joseph Campau to the end of the line, downtown at Broadway Street. From there they would cross the street to Haley's department store and go to the third floor where the fabric was sold. Their mother had promised each of the girls they could pick out the material for their new dress.

"When is the streetcar coming?" Laura asked, pulling at her white gloves.

"Any minute now," May Ford answered.

"Come on, Laura, let's clap," Patsy said.

Patsy and Laura clapped their hands together and then clapped to each other, left hand to left hand, once again clapped their hands together, then clapped to each other, right hand to right hand, all while they chanted, "Who stole the cookie from the cookie jar? Number one stole the cookie from the cookie jar. Who me? Yes, you. Couldn't be! Then who? Number two stole the cookie from the cookie jar . . ."

Jean stood to the side watching and listening. "Number three . . . number four . . . number five . . ." Then she tapped Patsy on the arm and said, "I w-w-wa, let me play, too!"

"But she can't say the words," Laura said, still clapping.

"Here, Jean," Patsy said. "You clap with Laura and I'll say the words."

Jean took her turn with Laura while Patsy and Laura kept up the chant, "Who stole the cookie from the cookie jar? Number six stole the cookie from the cookie jar. Who me? Yes, you. Couldn't be! Then who . . ."

Annie May looked up at their mother and asked. "Mama, who took the cookies?"

"There're no cookies, honey. It's just a game."

"Can we get cookies?" she asked, pointing to the bakery across the street.

"Not today, the streetcar will be here any minute now."

For the shopping trip downtown, the girls

wore cotton dresses with gathered skirts over starched white petticoats. May Ford wore a straight-line navy-blue linen dress and a small-brimmed straw hat. All five of them wore white cotton gloves. They stood out from the passersby who were dressed in work clothes or ordinary day outfits.

The clapping stopped.

"M-m-m-ama, it's too hot to wear gloves," Jean stammered, turning away from Laura. She started pulling them off.

"Keep them on, Jean," their mother said in a low voice. "A young lady always wears white gloves when she goes downtown."

"And church, too," Patsy added.

"Can we—*may* we have our gum now?" Laura asked, correcting herself.

Their mother made it a practice to hand out chewing gum to the children before they boarded the streetcar. It was the only time she approved of gum chewing. She explained it was to keep their stomachs settled as the car rocked side to side on the track. She reached inside her handbag and pulled out a little tin box.

"Don't chew like a cow," she said as she
passed out a square of gum to each of the girls.

When the streetcar arrived, their mother took
Annie May's hand and started up the steps.
"Patsy," she said. And Patsy knew just what to
do. She grabbed hands with Laura and Jean and
led them up the steps after their mother. They
walked past the motorman, who was seated at
the front, and toward the conductor, who sat
at the center of the car. They would each pay a
nickel to the conductor when it was time to get
off. They would drop the coins into a metal box
through a slit in the top, and only then would
he open the door so they could leave. But for
now, May Ford and Annie sat in two seats facing
forward next to a row of three seats facing the
aisle. She motioned with her head for Patsy and
the girls to take those seats, Patsy in the middle
and Laura and Jean on either side of her. The
seats were really benches made out of slats of
wood. They were plain but clean.

Patsy looked around the streetcar. There were
ladies, both colored and white, sitting nearby
who were also wearing white gloves. There
were Polish women with their heads covered

35

in bright, flowery babushkas. There were men in overalls carrying lunch pails. And then it was happening again—one thing Patsy always noticed when they took the streetcar downtown. Some of the people stared at her and her sisters, Doug, too, when he came along with them. And they especially stared at her mother. Especially May Ford. Laura noticed, too, on this ride. She said to Jean, "They're staring at Mama's hat!"

"M-m-m-m-mama, why are they staring at your hat?" Jean asked.

"Shush now, girls," their mother said.

But Patsy knew they were not staring at her hat. Strangers on the streetcar were staring at their mother because her skin was light. She looked white. She was not brown-skinned like Doug and her daughters. No one ever said anything directly to the children or their mother. But Patsy knew why they stared.

One time, on another ride, Patsy thought the people sitting in the row of seats directly behind them were whispering about them. She heard the words "yellow woman," "brown babies," "black-skinned man." Patsy had asked her mother if those people were talking about her.

May Ford turned and looked the people square in the eye. Then she turned back and said to Patsy, "No baby, they have better things to talk about."

This time on the ride downtown, something else caught Patsy's attention. She noticed the smell of something familiar. It was the same strong scent that came from the Yablonskis' kitchen on Easter Sunday, wafting out of their stove and in through the open window in her parents' bedroom. Smoked kielbasa and *kapusta*—sausage and sauerkraut—that's what she smelled. She leaned forward, sniffed, and let her nose take her to the source of that smell. She found it. There was a group of three men, men from the "old country," her mother would say. They sat in the rear of the streetcar, on the back bench. They held their boxes and suitcases wrapped in blankets and quilts on their laps and on the floor against their feet. It sounded to Patsy like they were speaking Polish. She couldn't understand what they were saying, but it sounded like some of the words she often heard coming from the Yablonskis' house.

First one and then all three of the men stood

up. They dragged their bags to where the conductor stood. When the car came to a halt at the next stop, two of the men put their nickels in the metal box and then started toward the steps. The conductor opened the door, but when the third man kept walking without paying the nickel, he closed the door right away.

"Nickel, please," the conductor said in a loud, strong voice.

The man said something to his friends in Polish. The two men who had paid their money replied in Polish and started down the steps, but the conductor explained, "I can't open the door until your buddy pays his fare."

More Polish. One man said, "No money."

"He cannot leave the streetcar until he pays his fare."

"Two of us go. He has no money."

"Who's going to pay his fare? He can't leave until he pays the nickel," the conductor said one more time.

The first two men were on the steps. The door was closed. They looked up at the conductor. The man with no money looked frightened.

Patsy looked down in her mother's lap as she

clicked open her pocketbook. She pulled out her change purse and took out a nickel. She put it in Patsy's hand and told her to put it in the metal box. Patsy started to get up and then she hesitated. "Go on, now," May said.

Patsy walked up to the conductor and deposited the coin. "Here's a nickel," she said.

The conductor opened the door.

The third man turned toward Patsy and nodded his head. Then all three of the men left the streetcar. Patsy went back to her seat. The conductor motioned to the motorman, and the streetcar lurched forward.

Amid the murmurs and grunts in the seats, Patsy heard two of the women in the babushkas speak to each other in Polish. *Kto ma dodatkowe niklu w tych dniach?* She caught the word *niklu* and thought it must mean nickel. They were saying something about the nickel. Other passengers spoke in English—"I didn't know what that conductor was going to do." "Nice lady." "Humph, she just thinks she's white. That Polish fella had that nickel. I know he did." "Oh, Hattie . . ."

Patsy looked over at their mother. Jean did, too. Laura leaned forward and said, "Mama—"

"Hush," their mother said, cutting off Laura before she could say more. Looking straight ahead she said, "Just let it go, girls. Just let it go."

3

Tickets to Clarksville

Patsy, Laura, and Jean found it hard to keep up
with their mother's brisk pace after they crossed
Joseph Campau and began the walk down
Halleck Street toward home. The midday sun
beat down on them. Wet circles grew larger on
their dresses under the arms. The girls started
dripping sweat down the sides of their temples
and down their necks. The more they sweated,
the more Patsy could catch the scent of their
mother's perfume they'd put on that morning.

May Ford carried a sleeping Annie in her left
arm, resting the child against her hip, her small
head lying on May's shoulder, and a large packet
wrapped in brown paper and tied with string in
the other arm. "Hurry along, girls, and keep up,"
their mother said as they approached Maine
Street. They still had three long blocks to walk
to make it home.

41

Patsy grabbed her sisters' hands and pulled them forward. "Let's go," she said.

"M-m-m-mama . . . I'm tired. It's hot," Jean whined, pulling back. Patsy gave her arm a mild yank as she pulled them ahead.

"Why do we have to go to Clarksville?" Laura asked.

"I just want to make sure your grandma and your aunts are all right," she answered. "They say everything's fine, but I want to see for myself. They had a flood down there last winter. The Cumberland River that flows past town seems to flood every ten years or so. But this flood was bad, worse than most folks can remember—the water rose to over sixty feet."

Laura gasped.

"I d-d-d . . ." Jean tried to get the words out.

"She doesn't wanna go," Laura interrupted.

"Laura, goodness knows, let your sister speak for herself," their mother said.

"But she can't."

"She can if you just let her."

Annie May popped her head up and looked around. "Good," their mother said. "I can put you down now." She stood the youngest on her feet and then smoothed out both of their dresses.

"I wanna see the fud, mama. What's the fud?" Annie May asked.

"It's flood, baby. Flood. That's when the water from the river comes over onto the dry land. And you won't be seeing it. It's all gone now. Been gone a long time," she said as she took Annie's hand and continued the walk home. She stepped at a slower pace now.

Patsy looked up at the street sign—MacKay—when they got to the corner. "Two more blocks to home," she said out loud.

By the time they reached the next street, Arlington, their mother's pace had slowed even more. Yet, Patsy still had to pull her sisters to help them keep up. "Stop pulling! Mama, Patsy's pulling my arm," Laura said.

"Keep up now, girls," the mother replied.

As they approached Goddard, Patsy could hear the muffled *hee-haw* sound of their father's saw. "Hear Daddy's saw? Almost home," she said to Jean and Laura. They crossed the street. Patsy noticed their mother picked up her pace as they approached the second house off the corner; it was the Williamses' place. She tugged her sisters along.

Again, Laura said to Patsy, "Stop pu—"

"Shhh!" May turned her head and shushed the girl.

There was yelling—a man and a woman. Patsy recognized the man's voice: it was Mr. Williams. She couldn't tell if the woman was Mrs. Williams or not. And she couldn't make out what they were saying. "Lord have mercy," their mother muttered as they hurried past the house. "Keep going, girls. Keep your eyes straight ahead," their mother said. Neither Patsy nor her sisters looked over at the Williamses' house. The man's voice got louder. It sounded like the woman was crying. There was the sound of glass breaking. The woman screamed . . . then there was silence.

May picked up Annie, and she and the girls hurried down the street. The sound of the *hee-haw* from their father's saw was loud and clear now. When they reached the Chambers' house, the house next door, their dog Pointo met them at the driveway and started barking. They were home.

"Don't move 'til I say so. I don't want to stick
you with one of these pins," May Ford cautioned
Patsy as she pinned the pleats in place around
her waist and adjusted the fabric over the dress
she still had on underneath. During the trip
downtown to Halcy's department store earlier
that day, she let the older girls pick out their
own fabric: Patsy wanted a sky-blue cotton
organdy. Laura chose a pink handkerchief linen
that their mother liked so much she bought
an extra yard for Annie's dress. Jean had
announced on the streetcar that she wanted a
yellow dress made out of dotted Swiss. They
scoured the entire third floor until their mother
finally found it. Up against the wall in a corner,
May noticed a bolt of fabric with small white
raised dots on yellow batiste: the dotted Swiss
fabric.

Now at home, there was fabric laid out all
over the dining room—on the table, on the floor,
draped across chairs. May sat at the treadle
sewing machine and Patsy stood next to her.
"Turn a little this way," she said, moving Patsy to
the right.

"When are you going to start my dress?" Laura called out from the piano in the living room. It was an upright model that Douglas Ford had bought from a customer a few years back. Laura was seated on the bench, practicing her scales. Annie was perched beside her.

"You're next," their mother answered. "Just hold your horses. Keep practicing your scales— you girls have your piano lessons this evening. I'll be ready for you in no time."

Annie May started banging on the piano keys. "I'm playing scales, too, Mama," she announced.

"Mama, make her stop!" Laura pleaded while finishing a run of notes.

"She can practice, too," May said. "She'll start her lessons before you know it. Let her make music with you."

"But it doesn't sound like mu—"

"Hush now!" their mother said, cutting her off.

Patsy winced as May took the pleated organdy from around her middle. One of the pins had indeed stuck her. "Sorry, baby," their mother said as she picked up a needle and thread and, with long running stitches, began basting the skirt to the top of the dress. Patsy sat down at the dining room table. She was making a dress, too, but not at the sewing machine. She was hand-stitching a dress for Annie May's doll, using scraps of organdy left over from her own dress. Annie came over from the piano and stood next to Patsy, watching as she took up her needle and thread. In no time, she had sewn the front and back bodice pieces together. She was starting to sew the top of the dress to the skirt when May called Patsy over to her.

"Are you ready for one more fitting?" May asked as she turned to Patsy.

Patsy smiled. "Yes, Mama," she said. She put down the unfinished doll's dress to go stand by her mother.

Annie May whined, "No, Patsy! Finish the dress for my dolly!"

"Annie, stop whining! She'll finish the dress before we leave for Clarksville. She's almost finished now," May said.

May took a piece of tailor's chalk and marked the hem on Patsy's dress and then marked where the buttonholes would be hand-sewn along the back. She even pinned on a satin ribbon sash that would be tied in a bow under the back buttons. Patsy did not have to look in a mirror to know that the dress fit her perfectly. She could tell by the way it hung from her shoulders and then billowed out in full pleats from her waist to a few inches below her knees.

There was not much breeze coming in through the dining room window as May hovered over the sewing machine. Every few minutes, she stopped to fan herself with the paper she had sketched the girls' dresses on. Patsy intently watched her put the final stitches on the dress. Her mother's foot, firmly resting on the wide, wrought-iron foot pedal, pushed down first toe then heel—back and forth—until she had a steady rocking rhythm going. Patsy saw the tense look on her mother's face: it was hard work pressing the treadle that moved the belt and turned the wheel, pushing the needle in and out of the fabric.

Several minutes later the sewing machine stopped. May cut the thread and held up the dress.

"Ahh!" Laura gasped. She jumped up from the piano and ran into the dining room. "Mama, I want one just like that," she said standing next to the outfit.

"Uh-uh, you get your own," Patsy answered.

"But, I—"

"That's enough, girls," their mother said. She held up a drawing.

"Here's what your dress will look like, Laura." She pointed to a loose sheath with a ruffle at the hem and around the neck. Annie's was the same except her dress had a gathered skirt at the waist.

"M-m-m-mama, how do you sew so fast?" Jean asked.

Patsy looked behind her. Jean had been standing quietly and watching from the other side of the room, in the doorway to her parents' bedroom.

"Honey, I've told you, before," she answered, "I was one piece away from getting my diploma at Tennessee State University and my teaching certificate in home economics when I married your father. There's not much I didn't learn about sewing, crocheting, embroidery . . ." Her voice trailed off. Then she repeated herself, "One piece away." She looked at Patsy, Laura, then Jean and said, "Let that be a lesson to you girls: always finish what you start!"

"But you were a teacher in Clarksville, Mama," Patsy said. "You said you were one of the teachers at the colored school."

"I was the *only* teacher, baby. It was a one-room schoolhouse for the colored children in town. They let me teach, all right. But that doesn't change the fact that I didn't have my certificate. I couldn't teach up here once I married your father and came to Detroit. No, the lesson's the same, and you girls remember it—finish what you start."

"May!" Douglas Ford strode in through the kitchen. "I'm gonna get those tickets now. Where're my girls? Who's ready to go with me to the train station?"

Annie May and Jean ran up to him. He grabbed them both and lifted them in his arms.

"I'm ready, Daddy!" Patsy answered.

"Me too! Can I go, Mama?" Laura asked.

"No, baby, I need you here to fit this dress," May said to Laura. She plopped down on the floor and pouted.

"You'll get to the train station soon enough,"

their mother said. Then, turning to Patsy, she added, "Go on now. You go on with your father and get some good seats for us."

"Oh, and Douglas, the girls have their piano lessons this evening. So don't stay too long," May said to her husband as he turned to leave through the kitchen.

"Right before the trip?" he asked without looking back.

"They need their lessons. Patsy has to be ready to play this fall when Sunday school starts up again. Anyway, Mrs. Lewis enjoys seeing the girls . . ."

"That's because they're her only students," he murmured as he walked out the back door, Patsy right behind him.

ᔕ

Train leaving for Chicago now boarding at track number 19.

In the background, the announcement bellowed over the public address system in the Michigan Central Station. Someone bumped up against Patsy as she almost ran to keep up with her father's long strides. He moved quickly and deliberately through the crowd in the train station.

"Daddy, don't walk so fast," she pleaded.

"You've got to keep moving in this kind of crowd," he said. "Otherwise you'll never get through. Come on, now." He grabbed her gloved hand and kept moving.

Last call for train stopping in Toledo, Cincinnati, Louisville, Clarksville, and Nashville. Boarding at track number 23. All aboard!

"Clarksville, Daddy! Is that our train?" she asked, almost yelling to be heard over the crowd.

"Yes, baby. That's it. All the way down to Clarksville, Tennessee . . ."

Patsy looked around the station. It was the biggest building she could remember ever being in: rows of tall, wide marble columns two stories high. Shiny marble floors. Long wooden benches in the main waiting room, longer than the pews at church and crowded with people and their suitcases. There was a gift shop, a shoeshine parlor, a florist stand. She looked straight ahead beneath a gigantic brass clock— the windows of the ticket offices.

"Look Daddy! Over there—that's where we buy the tickets!" She pointed.

"Mmm-hmm," he said.

Patsy started walking toward the ticket counters, but her father pulled her in a different direction.

"Daddy, it's over there."

"I see where it is, child. Come with me."

Patsy followed her father past the newsstand, a drugstore, and a barbershop.

Express train to Pittsburgh, Pennsylvania, now boarding on track number 7. Last call for Chicago, track number 19. All aboard!

"Where're we going, Daddy?"

Douglas Ford didn't say a word. He held her hand as they weaved through the crowd. When they turned a final corner, Patsy knew right away where her father had taken her. Directly ahead of them was a huge lunch counter and soda fountain, with tall cushioned stools and a gleaming marble countertop.

"Daddy!" she shrieked.

"I promised you a strawberry soda now, didn't I?" he asked.

And he had, in the hottest part of the

afternoon, as he drove them to the train station in one of the Ford Model A pickup trucks he used in his business.

Wearing the same white gloves and dress she had worn downtown that morning, Patsy wiped the sweat off of her forehead with the back of her hand.

Her father looked over at her in the passenger's seat and said, "A nice cold strawberry soda would taste pretty good right now."

"Sure would," Patsy answered.

"Then I think that's what we'll have—there's a soda fountain at the train station . . ."

Pullman car bound for New York City now boarding on track 5.

Before Patsy could step onto the footrail under the counter and pull herself up onto the stool, her father had swooped her up in his arms, lifted her gently, and placed her on the leather-cushioned stool.

"Whoa!" She giggled.

"There, how's that?" he asked.

"Thanks, Daddy."

As Patsy straightened and arranged the

skirt of her dress over the stool and folded her gloves neatly on her lap, her father ordered two strawberry sodas "with extra whipped cream."

The bright-pink sodas were the biggest Patsy had ever seen. As she dipped her spoon in deep, a bit of the ice cream and whipped cream spilled over the tall glass and onto the counter.

"Don't worry about that little mess," her father said. "Just take your time. Enjoy your soda and cool off."

∽

Last call for Pittsburgh on track number 7. All aboard!

Patsy and her father had finished their treats and now they stood at the ticket window, directly under the big brass clock.

"Five first-class tickets to Clarksville, Tennessee, please, departing Wednesday, July 14, returning Wednesday, July 21," Douglas Ford said. "Morning departure," he added.

The clerk looked over at Patsy and then up at her father. He peered over the rim of his glasses and said, "You know you'll have to change trains at the Cincinnati station."

"I know the protocol," her father answered.

"Cincinnati? Why Cincinnati?" Patsy asked him.

"You still want first-class tickets?" the clerk asked.

"Yes," Douglas answered curtly.

The clerk shook his head and then handed him the five tickets. "No morning departures that day. The earliest departure is at 2:05 p.m."

Her father paid the clerk. As they turned and walked away, Patsy asked him, "Why are we changing trains in Cincinnati? Is it a special train?"

"Honey—," he started to say something and abruptly stopped speaking. Then he finished the sentence. "It's a long ride to Clarksville, child," he said, "a long ride."

4

The Colored Car

Patsy could not remember her last train ride,
but she was looking forward to this one. In the
few days since going with her father to purchase
the tickets and now, arriving at the train
station, her mother had delighted the girls with
stories about their last train trip to Clarksville,
Tennessee. She told them that Doug was four
years old, Patsy was two, Laura was just a babe
in arms, and Jean and Annie May had not even
been born yet. She explained how porters took
the luggage to the baggage car. She said the
conductor checked everyone's ticket and made
sure the train ran on time. She described the
first-class train car with its fancy, upholstered
seats and beautiful carpet down the aisle. She
named all of the different foods available right
there in the train car—dumplings stuffed with
chicken or roast beef, tea sandwiches, petit

fours, fresh fruit compote. By the time the family arrived at the Michigan Central Station that afternoon—except for Doug who stayed home to unload a haul of wood—Patsy's stomach was feeling a little funny, she was so excited.

Douglas Ford went on ahead with the porter to get their luggage packed in the baggage car. May and the girls made a stop in the gift shop where she bought each of them a bag of peppermints for the trip. Patsy popped a peppermint in her mouth right away to help settle her stomach.

Train leaving for Toledo, Cincinnati, Louisville, Clarksville, and Nashville now boarding at track number 23.

"Come along, girls," their mother said, holding Annie May in one arm and grabbing Jean's hand with the other. Patsy and Laura followed her quick steps to meet their father at their train on track number 23. With train cars lined up on track after track, the smell of soot in the air got heavy and made Patsy's nose itch. She coughed into her glove. Laura and Jean started coughing, too.

"Put your handkerchief up to your nose,

girls," May Ford instructed the sisters. "It will make it easier for you to breathe 'til we get onto the train."

When the coughing did not subside, May assured them, "They have air filters on the train cars. You won't notice the soot and smoke from these steam engines not nearly as much."

Their father was standing by the first-class passenger car, beckoning them with his hand to hurry on up.

"All right, now, there's your father," their mother said.

All of the girls, except Annie May, ran up to meet him. Jean reached him first, and he scooped her up in his arms. Then just as quickly, when Patsy and Laura reached him, he put Jean down and hugged all three tightly. "You be good girls."

"We will, Daddy, we will."

"And mind your mother. Help her with baby Annie May."

"We will, Daddy!"

Last call for Toledo, Columbus, Cincinnati, Louisville, Clarksville, and Nashville. Boarding at track number 23.

May Ford and Annie were standing with the other girls now. Douglas kissed his wife on the forehead. He kissed Annie May on the cheek. Then he helped each one onto the train car. May showed the girls to their seats. They left their seats and pressed their faces up against the windows looking for their father. May stood behind them.

"Bye-bye, Daddy! Bye!"

All aboard!

There were two seats to a row. Patsy had the window seat and Laura sat next to the aisle. Jean sat in a window seat in the row behind them next to her mother, who was holding Annie May in her lap. Their father stood on the platform as the train slowly moved along the tracks. Patsy, sitting now, kept her face pressed against the window and waved until he was out of sight.

The conductor entered the car. "Tickets ready, please," he announced. Patsy turned her head and looked in the space between their two seats. She watched as her mother reached into her pocketbook and pulled out the five tickets. When he stopped by her seat, he punched a hole in each one. "Enjoy the ride," he said, without looking at either May or the girls, and moved on to the next row of passengers. He was a white man, and Patsy noticed that he looked the other white passengers in the eye and smiled when he punched their train tickets. But for the few other colored passengers in that first-class car, he did not look at them and he did not smile.

శా

The train car was just as May Ford had described it to the girls. Patsy and Laura giggled as they bounced up and down upon the plush red velvet cushions on their upholstered seats. "Settle down, girls," May said. "We've got a long ride ahead of us. It'll be evening before we reach Columbus."

Patsy spread the skirt of her dress across the width of her seat and placed both feet on the footrest bolted to the floor in front of her. She folded her hands in her lap, along with her bag of peppermints, and looked out the window. Laura tried to spread her dress over her cushion as well, but her dress did not have the same full skirt and she could not do it. Her legs were too short to reach the footrest.

"Mama," Laura pouted, "I want a dress like Patsy's! My dress won't fit over the cushion."

"Shhh. Your dress is fine," their mother said.

Out of the corner of her eye, Patsy saw a white handkerchief on the red-and-green floral-patterned rug in the aisle. She turned and asked her sister, "Is that your handkerchief?"

Laura looked straight ahead and answered, "I don't need it."

Patsy turned and, looking between their two seats, said, "Mama, Laura dropped her handkerchief and she won't pick it up!"

"But I don't need it anymore," Laura explained before her mother could say a word. "It doesn't smell bad in here. It doesn't make me cough."

"There's good ventilation in this car, that's for sure. They keep the air clean," their mother said. "But pick up your handkerchief."

Laura did as she was told. Patsy turned back in her seat. The two sisters looked out the window as they passed the small cities and towns outside of Detroit.

May said, "Girls, your father and his drivers deliver wood to houses in all of these towns we're passing through now."

An hour later, Patsy looked up when a waiter, a dark-skinned man like her father, who was wearing a white jacket and black bow tie, entered their car. He was pushing a cart covered with a white tablecloth. On top of the cart was a large silver tray filled with cookies and sandwiches.

As he moved closer to their seats, May Ford said, "Waiter, tea sandwiches for my girls and me, please."

The waiter made a slight bow and placed a linen napkin in each girl's lap and gave the mother one napkin to share with Annie May. The sisters smiled as they watched him use silver tongs to place three small sandwiches, filled with butter, lettuce, and cucumber slices, on each napkin.

"Enjoy your food," the waiter said, bowing again.

"Oooh, M-m-mama, these sandwiches are pretty!" Jean said.

Laura asked, "Mama, are these the same kind of sandwiches you had on the train the last time you went to Clarksville?"

"Yes, dear," she answered.

"I don't wanna sandwich, I wanna cookie," Annie May said.

"No cookies, baby. Now girls, enjoy your meal."

When she was almost finished eating, Patsy turned and said, "Mama—"

"Don't talk with your mouth full," her mother said.

Patsy chewed and swallowed. "Mama, the ticket man said we stop in Cincinnati."

"Yes, baby . . . You know, there's a big new terminal there, the Union Terminal. We'll see it for sure. Now girls, everyone hand me your napkins so they don't end up on the floor."

Patsy was going to ask more questions, but May was busy folding the napkins and Annie May was fussing in her lap. Patsy turned and settled in her seat. Rocked by with the gentle motion of the train car, she fell asleep.

ᔓ

Half-asleep, half-awake, Patsy heard the long, high pitch of the train whistle blowing. She looked over at Laura, still dozing next to her.

"M-m-m-mama, w-w-w-what's the whistle for?" Jean, wide-awake, asked her mother.

"Next stop Columbus!" Patsy could barely hear the conductor calling out in the next car.

The conductor walked into their car, announcing, "Next stop Columbus!"

"You see?" May answered. "It just means we're coming to a train station. We'll take on more people and keep going."

"We passed Toledo already?" Patsy turned and asked.

May smiled. "You were sound asleep through that stop," she answered.

"So, we're in Columbus now?" Patsy asked.

"Just about," she answered.

"Mama," Patsy said, "the ticket man said we'll change trains in Cincinnati."

"Yes, we will, he was right about that."

"C-c-c-can I have another sandwich?" Jean asked.

"*May* I have another sandwich," their mother corrected her.

"M-m-m-may I?" Jean repeated.

"May I have one, too?" Patsy asked.

"I wanna cookie this time," Annie May said.

65

"When the waiter comes through again, you may each have one more sandwich," their mother said.

Right then the train arrived at the Columbus station. As soon as the train stopped, Laura woke up. She leaned toward the window.

"It's getting dark. Where are we?" she asked Patsy.

"The conductor just said we're in Columbus," Patsy answered.

Patsy and Laura watched as people both left the train and entered the car. The conductor stood on the platform. Another man in a uniform helped passengers step up into the train car.

"Who's that other man, Mama?" Laura asked.

"That's a porter, baby. They help people onto the train. A porter helped your father take our luggage to the baggage car . . ."

"W-w-w-when are w-we going to get there, M-m-mama?" Jean asked.

"I told you girls this was going to be a very long train ride. We've still got stops in Cincinnati and Louisville before we get to Clarksville early next morning."

Patsy watched as her mother reached into her

pocketbook. She pulled out a small ball of twine and handed it to Patsy between the seats.

"Here, Patsy—unroll this ball of string, knot the end, and you and Laura can play Cat's Cradle."

"Oooh! Cat's Cradle! Thank you, Mama," Laura said.

"I w-w-want to play C-c-cat's C-c-cradle, too!" Jean said, sulking.

"Here, I have something better for you." May reached back into her pocketbook and pulled out a small chalk doll with painted hair and clothes.

Jean grinned. "Thank you, M-m-mama," she said, and settled back in her seat with the doll.

"Where's my doll?" Annie May asked.

"You just put your head on my shoulder. It's time for you to go to sleep," her mother said.

Patsy hurriedly tied the knot and made a string circle. She spread her hands within the circle and then made a loop around each hand. She reached each middle finger across to the opposite loop and pulled the string onto the finger. Laura then took her thumb and index finger and pinched the string at the two places where the loops crossed on Patsy's hand. She pulled them out, and—swinging her hand under Patsy's hands—moved the entire piece onto her hands.

All aboard! Next stop Cincinnati!

Patsy and Laura played with the string until the waiter returned, about an hour outside Columbus, with the sandwich cart.

❧

Patsy watched as a different conductor entered their train car and announced, "Next stop Cincinnati!" He looked up and down the rows of seats and walked over to where her mother sat. "Are these your babies? Your young 'uns?" he asked brusquely, looking over at May and then at the girls.

Once again, Patsy knew why he asked: her mother's light skin was almost as white as the conductor's and not like the color of her four brown-skinned girls.

May looked him straight in the eye. "Yes, these are my children," she answered.

"We're comin' up on Cincinnati," he continued. "You'll need to change cars."

"We'll be ready," she said.

"Where are we going?" Laura asked.

"You said there's a new train station in Cincinnati. Can we go see it, Mama?" Patsy asked.

"We'll just have time to look at it from the outside, at the most. But it's so dark out; I don't know how much we'll even be able to see. There probably won't be time for much else. But we'll see," the mother answered.

The train had stopped and the conductor announced from the platform, "Cincinnati Union Station!"

"All right, girls," May Ford instructed, "gather up your things. Get up, now. Put on your gloves. Make sure you have your handkerchiefs. Do you have any peppermints left? No, I didn't think so. Come now, let's go."

Patsy and her sisters stood and did as they were told: They put on their white gloves and held tight to their handkerchiefs. With baby Annie May in her arm, their mother led them off of the train. That same conductor was standing there as they left the car. He directed them and the other colored passengers who were leaving their train cars, "This way to the colored car."

"What's the colored car, Mama?" Patsy asked.

"Patsy, you take Laura's hand," their mother said. "Follow close to me."

It was almost midnight but the heat was still stifling. With Annie still in her arm, May wiped her forehead and the back of her neck with her handkerchief. Then, she took Jean's hand. They walked into the crowd of people on the platform, some were standing, some walking, some seated on benches.

"Here we go girls, we won't have to walk too far, I don't think," their mother said.

They walked up to a car. May Ford looked up. Patsy followed her mother's gaze. Above the steps to the train car was a sign with the word COLORED on it.

Last call for Louisville, Clarksville, and Nashville!

"This is it. Patsy, you and Laura go on in now," their mother said, "I'm right behind you."

They stood behind a line of passengers, all colored, who were getting on the train car.

Patsy led her sister into the car. She stopped

in the doorway. It took just a few seconds for her to take it all in—the floor was bare and worn and there were rows of old wooden seats. There was no upholstery, no cushions, no curtains. A rusty, pot-bellied stove was situated in the middle of the car. There was soot in the air and she started to cough. She looked up at her mother and said, "Mama, this car's dirty . . . our dresses will get dirty. Let's go back to the other one."

"We can't do that. Come on and make the best of it."

As May Ford led the other girls to their seats, Patsy stood in the doorway.

"But it's dirty, Mama. Let's go back to the other car. Why couldn't we just stay in that car?" Patsy asked. "There were other people staying in that car."

"Take your seat, Patsy. This is where we'll be until we get to Clarksville," her mother said.

Patsy turned and went back down the stairs and stood on the platform. The mother looked at the other sisters and commanded, "Stay right here, girls." Then she joined Patsy on the platform and grabbed her daughter's arm.

"Patsy, what's gotten into you? You can't go running off like that. Now get back on the train!"

Patsy pulled away. "Mama, that train car smells. It's dirty. It made me cough. The seats are all crowded together. There're no cushions on the seats . . . How can we ride all the way to Clarksville in that colored car?"

"Oh, sweetheart, it won't be so bad. You'll fall asleep. We'll be there before you know it, bright and early in the morning."

All aboard!

"No, Mama—get Laura and Jean and the baby. Let's go back . . ." Patsy's voice was shaking.

"Patsy, now stop it. We cannot go back to the other car. We have to ride in this car. *We have to ride in the colored car!*"

"But why, Mama, why?" Patsy's eyes were filled with tears.

"Listen baby—when we leave Cincinnati, we'll be in the South. In the North, where we live, colored people and white people can sit on any train they want. In the South—Kentucky, Tennessee, Alabama, Georgia, all the southern states—they want colored people to sit on the train with other colored people."

Patsy's mouth dropped open. "That's why there were mostly colored people getting off of our train? But I saw some white people getting off, too."

"They probably had business or family in Cincinnati," her mother explained. "But if they didn't, they didn't have to leave their seats."

"Let's get a move on!" The gruff voice behind them belonged to the conductor.

"We'll be on presently," May Ford answered him.

She turned to Patsy and held out her hand. "Come on, now."

Patsy stood firm. "I don't want to sit in that colored car!"

"Please, child, come on."

Patsy looked up and saw Laura and Jean looking out the window. She wanted to be with her sisters, but not in the colored car.

"Everybody in the car!" It was the conductor again.

"Come on, Patsy!" Her mother's voice was firm now, no longer pleading. Sweat was beading up on her forehead.

"If you can't get her up in that car, I will," the conductor said, reaching for Patsy's arm.

"Don't touch my daughter, sir," May Ford said sternly.

The conductor stepped back and looked May straight in the eyes. Veins were bulging out on his forehead. His white face seemed to turn almost purple.

"What did you say to me?" he demanded.

"I said don't touch my daughter." May's voice was cold. Patsy stepped away from the conductor's reach. She was shaking. By that point, people walking by on the platform—colored and white—had stopped and were watching.

"Oh yes, but I will touch your daughter. And I will drag her onto that car if I have to because I've got a train to run! Now you take this little picka—"

Right then, from behind, Patsy felt the firm grasp of two massive hands lift her off the ground.

"Daddy? Daddy is that you?" Patsy asked.

"Let me help here, sir," the man said.

Patsy looked over at the man's face. It was not

her father. It was a tall, light-skinned colored
man. He had on a dark-blue cap. The words
"Pullman Porter" were etched in brass in the
middle of the cap.

The porter lifted her up and carried her up
the steps. He spoke gently. "Let's get you on up
this train. You'll be fine. You'll have a good ride, I
promise you."

Patsy saw her mother hurry up behind them.
"Thank you, sir, thank you so much."

The porter put Patsy down in a seat right
behind her sisters. "How's this?" he asked.
Patsy just nodded her head. There were tears
streaming down her cheeks.

"That's fine," her mother said, a little
flustered, as she reached into her pocketbook.

"No, please," he said as May tried to hand him
a dollar coin. "I'm more than happy to help." He
tipped his cap to her and then to Patsy. "Have a
good trip," he said and left the train.

*All aboard for Louisville, Clarksville, and
Nashville!*

Patsy sat in the wooden seat by the window.
May Ford sat next to her with Annie May sitting
in the aisle seat. Patsy felt her mother's arm

wrapped tightly around her shoulder. She raised her gloved hand to wipe the tears from her face, but she noticed some soot on her glove. She took it off and used the back of her hand instead.

Jean and Laura were peeking at Patsy and their mother through the space between their two seats.

May furrowed her brow and gave the two girls a stern look. They quickly turned around.

"We'll be in Clarksville before you know it," May said to Patsy. "Grandma Jackson will be so glad to see you and your sisters. And I bet you more than anything there'll be an apple pie on the table. You'll be able to smell it as soon as we walk in the door. Mama always bakes an apple pie when there's company coming . . ."

"She raised those girls to think they're too good for the colored car . . ."

Patsy leaned forward and looked past her mother and Annie May. It was the woman in the next aisle muttering just loud enough for them to hear.

"Bet they know different now, don't they."

Patsy looked up at her mother. May's face had turned red. She stood up and faced the woman.

"No one," Patsy's mother said in a firm voice, "*no one* tells me how to raise my children."

The woman didn't say another word. She turned her head and looked the other way.

As her mother sat back down, Patsy looked down at the folds in the skirt of her dress.

"Oh, Mama, look!" she whimpered. The soft organdy fabric hung over the side of the wooden seat. Patsy could see long, dark smudges all across the pale-blue gathers of her dress. She broke down into tears. She could barely speak. "Mama," she cried softly, "my dress is dirty!"

5

Clarksville, Tennessee

*Clarksville Station! Next stop Nashville. All
aboard!*

"Baby, we're here. Clarksville. Come on,
honey, let's go," May Ford said to Patsy as she
leaned close to her ear and touched her gently
on the shoulder.

Patsy opened her eyes and looked out the
window. It was morning now. They were at a
train station. People, colored and white, were
walking along the platform: some carrying
luggage, some standing empty-handed and
looking as if they were still waiting for someone
to arrive by train.

"Patsy, we have to get off now. We're in
Clarksville," her mother said again, her hand
still resting on her daughter's shoulder.

Patsy looked around the car and saw the
wood-burning stove and a few people, colored

passengers, still sitting on the wooden seats.
The odor of soot and smoke was still heavy
in the air. She coughed. And then Patsy
remembered: getting off the first-class train car
in Cincinnati, the conductor in a rage, the strong
arms of the Pullman porter carrying her to her
seat in the colored car. She looked down at her
dress, at the smudges of soot and dirt across
the folds of her skirt. *She was in the colored car.*
Patsy jumped up from her seat, brushing past
her mother. Her sisters stood in the doorway
and she rushed right by them as well, off the
train and onto the platform. She stood there,
looking away from the colored car and walking
toward the train station.

"Wait, Patsy," her mother said.

Patsy stopped and turned around.

"Let's find a porter and get our bags," her
mother said, leading Patsy and her sisters to the
baggage car.

Standing by the baggage car as the porter
unloaded their luggage onto a cart, Laura was
the first to notice: "Mama, look, over there."

She pointed in the direction of the station. On
the outside wall were water fountains. Each one

had a sign overhead, one that said Colored Only and the other that said Whites Only.

"Please take our bags to the taxi stand," May said to the porter, a colored man wearing overalls and a straw cap.

"Yes, ma'am," he replied, tipping his hat.

"Why do they put those signs over the water?" Laura asked her mother.

"Good Lord," her mother replied, shaking her head. "Welcome to Clarksville. We're in Tennessee now. We're in the South. Things are different here. We'll talk about it later."

"Can I have a drink from the colored fountain?" Laura asked.

"No baby, we'll have time for a nice cool drink once we get to Grandma Jackson's house," her mother said.

"W-w-what c-c-color is the w-water?" Jean asked.

"I want colored water, too!" Annie May said.

With a low, emotionless voice, Patsy said, "It's not colored *water.* That water fountain is for colored people to *drink* from. Right, mama?"

"Yes, dear, you're right," her mother answered

with a sigh. "Now, come along girls, don't let the porter get too far ahead of us."

Last call for Nashville, Tennessee. All aboard!

The porter had pushed the cart through the door into the train station and was standing at the door, holding it open, waiting for May Ford and the girls. May held Annie May in her left arm and held Jean's hand with her right hand. Laura and Patsy walked behind.

As they followed the porter to the taxi stand, Laura said, "Mama, this station is a lot smaller than the train station in Detroit."

"Yes, it is baby."

"I don't see any shops like in our train station. And there aren't many people here."

"It's a small town, honey. They don't need a great big train station."

The porter stopped his cart at the first car at the taxi stand. *Clarksville Taxi* was painted in yellow letters on the back and on the side of the black car.

May crouched down slightly and said to the taxi driver through the open passenger door window, "We want to go to 534 Franklin Street."

The driver, a white man, turned her way,

looked at her and the girls, then turned his head back. Still looking away from her, he said, "Don't go there."

"Where do you go?" May asked.

The driver pointed to the car ahead of him.

Patsy looked up ahead and saw a colored man sitting in a plain black car with no letters painted on it.

May was still leaning forward and looking at the taxi driver when the porter, head lowered and in a barely audible voice, said, "Ma'am, he's pointing to that jitney up ahead."

May turned and looked at the colored driver in the car several yards ahead of them. She straightened up and nodded to the porter. He headed to the jitney with their baggage.

"All right, girls, that man over there will take us to my mama's house."

～

First thing in the door, Patsy saw the apple pie on the dining room table when she, her mother, and sisters arrived at Grandmother Jackson's home. But the house did not smell like apple pie as her mother had assured her it would on the train. The house smelled like bleach.

While her grandmother passed rounds of kisses and hugs to each of the girls over and over again, all the while exclaiming, "You babies are a sight for sore eyes! Yes, indeed, a sight for sore eyes," Patsy was the first to actually start rubbing her eyes. Jean and Laura followed suit. Then as Grandma Jackson held Annie May up in her arms and fussed over how much each of the sisters had grown, Patsy noticed the baby was starting to heave. And before even her grandmother noticed what was about to happen, Annie May had vomited across the front of their grandmother's dress.

"Eee-uuuh!" Laura and Jean said in a chorus while Patsy backed off quietly into a corner of living room and sat down and watched the others.

"Well, bless her heart!" her grandmother exclaimed as she handed a now-crying Annie May over to her mother and went into the kitchen. "Let me just wipe off this dress . . . All this excitement and the long train ride has upset the poor child's stomach."

"I don't think it's the train ride, Mama," May Ford said holding Annie May in the doorway to the kitchen. "I think the smell of bleach around here has upset her stomach. Didn't you look at the girls rubbing their eyes?"

"Well, you know we didn't get any floodwater up in the house here, but we did get some water in the crawl space. I don't know if it was rainwater or river water, but I've been pouring bleach down in there just to make sure we don't get any mold or sickness comin' up here in the house," Grandma Jackson explained.

"Mama, the mold's dead, that's for sure. You must've poured some this morning?" she asked.

"Last night . . . I just didn't want to risk the girls being near any mold. The summer heat makes it smell worse than it really is. Come on now, let me see these babies again! Now don't you girls look pretty," she said as Laura and Jean ran into the kitchen. Patsy was still sitting in the big overstuffed chair in the living room.

"Where's Patsy?" the grandma asked. "Patsy, come on here in the kitchen. Let me see my oldest granddaughter . . ."

Patsy did not move.

"Patsy!" May Ford called.

Patsy slowly made her way to the kitchen. "May, you really sewed yourself up a storm now, didn't you? Patsy, that is such a pretty dress."

Patsy held up part of her skirt. "It got dirty," she said. "See?"

"On the train? My, my . . ."

"We had to change trains," Patsy said, almost whispering.

"Cincinnati," May explained.

"The train was dirty," Patsy said, looking down at the floor.

"Well, that happens sometimes," Grandma Jackson said while walking over to Patsy. She put her arm around her granddaughter. "But you're here now, and I'm so glad to see you."

Patsy rested her head against the grandmother's bosom and then burst into tears.

"Oh dear child," she exclaimed. "It's all right. Everything's all right. There's just too much excitement, is all," she said. She started walking Patsy toward the back door. "Let's go out in the yard and have some of that apple pie under the big tree. It's too hot in here. And Lord knows I did use too much bleach."

She turned toward the kitchen table. "May, cut up the pie and then bring it out on those small plates over there. Girls, help your mother bring out the silverware. Let Annie bring out the napkins. We'll just go outside and sit around the picnic table. We can catch a little breeze and cool off in the shade."

∽

Everyone sat outside around the big table, eating apple pie. They ate and listened as Grandma Jackson talked about the big flood.

" . . . it was worse than any flood I can remember in a long, long time," she said, putting her fork down on the table. "The pumping station was flooded out. Had to boil the water before we could drink it. All of Clarksville was vaccinated for typhoid fever. Hadn't heard of such a thing before. We're on high ground, here—same for your sisters—but—"

"So where are Addie and Pat?" May interrupted.

"Your sisters'll be by the house this evening. Don't you worry about that," Grandma answered. Then she continued, "So, in some parts of the city the river rose past sixty-five feet! You know? Some folks lost their houses, lost everything. They put the colored families, the ones that'd lost their homes, at the city hall; white families they put in the old post office."

Patsy looked up from her plate. "City hall?" she asked.

"Yes, child," the grandmother answered.

"Was it like the colored car on the train? Was it dirty?" Patsy asked.

"Well, honey, I don't suppose so. City hall, the post office, it didn't matter. They found room to take care of everybody that needed a place to stay."

Grandma Jackson ate more of her pie. She continued, "They even had to close down two or three of the fat roads . . ."

Laura giggled.

"W-w-w-what's a fat road?" Jean asked.

"That's just a wide road, like Davison or Dequindre back home," May Ford answered.

"Cars couldn't ride on them, so they traveled on those roads by boats. Now that was a sight to see!" their grandmother continued.

Jean and Laura were still eating. Patsy had

finished her pie and just moved what was left of the crust around on her plate. Annie May ran around the table laughing to herself.

"Makes me hot just watching that child run," May Ford said as she leaned back, fanning herself with her napkin.

"Full as a tick, that's what I am," Grandma Jackson said as she finished her pie and pushed her empty plate away from her on the picnic table.

Laura laughed and said, "Grandma talks funny!"

"Hush, now," their mother said.

"W-w-w-what's a tick?" Jean asked.

"It's a kind of a bug. A real little bug," May answered.

"May, when did Jean get that stutter?" Grandma Jackson asked.

"Just about a year ago. I don't have any idea what brought it on," May said.

"You know, I don't see these girls nearly enough. Goodness knows, I've just been up to Detroit twice since you were last here in '27. This is only the second time I've seen baby Annie May." She paused and then continued,

"Jean'll outgrow that stutter, I know she will. Sadie Lee Thompson's girl had a stutter and she outgrew it. So will Jean. It'll go away just like it came."

Laura and Jean jumped up from the table while their grandmother was talking. Patsy sat at the table and watched them chase Annie May around the tree.

"Don't you want to go play with your sisters?" the grandmother asked.

Patsy shook her head.

"Are you worried about your dress? I can get it clean in no time. It'll look better then new."

Patsy looked down at her plate.

"She'll be all right, Mama," May said. "It was a long trip. A long time on the train . . ."

૭

The next morning, still in her pajamas, Patsy sat on the floor outside the kitchen, leaning against the wall. She was listening to her mother and grandmother. When she came downstairs, they were already talking. They were not arguing. But Patsy could tell by the way her mother clipped her words and kept trying to keep her voice down to a whisper that she was not happy. And she could tell the two of them were talking about her.

"That child is just moping around the house," Grandma Jackson said. "Last night she acted like she didn't even know Addie and Pat . . ."

"Well, Mama, she's barely seen them—just once before—her entire life."

"You know what I mean."

"Well, it did get kinda ugly at the train station. I said some things that old conductor probably never heard come from a colored woman's mouth. Thank God that Pullman porter showed up when he did!" May said.

"You should've told her, May," Grandma Jackson said.

"Told her what, Mama?" May answered. "'Oh, Patsy, when we get to Cincinnati we move to a different train car because south of the Mason-Dixon Line colored folks are treated like second-class citizens?' Is that what you wanted me to tell her?"

"Oh, May . . ."

"I grew up knowing this life. It's not like that for these children . . ." May paused. "Maybe

I should've said something beforehand. But sometimes the best preparation is to just live through it. I did what I did, and she'll just have to find a way to handle it."

While Patsy sat outside the kitchen listening, Laura crawled up beside her. Patsy held her index finger up to her lips and mouthed, "Shhh!"

Laura said at the top of her voice, "Mama, Patsy's sitting outside the kitchen listening to you and Grandma talk!"

May Ford came outside the kitchen and looked down at both of them. "That's all right," she said. "We're not saying anything she shouldn't hear. Now, both of you, scoot! Go get washed and dressed! And put on your nice sundresses. We're going to do some visiting later on this afternoon."

༄

"Come on, girls. We're going for a little walk, see who's home. I want you to meet some of my friends from way back," May Ford said. She looked ready to stand up. They were all seated in the wicker chairs on the front porch: Annie

May and Patsy, Laura and Jean seated two to a chair.

"Walk?" Grandma Jackson asked. "Nonsense. I'll call up a jitney."

Turning to her mother, May said, "Jitney? We're just going a few blocks over."

"To the other side of Colored Town? In this heat? No, no, no, I won't have it," the grandmother said.

May chuckled, "You know, Mama, I've been away so long, I tried to get a taxi driver to bring us here yesterday morning. The man looked at me like I had lost my mind! Lord have mercy, I've forgotten so much about life down here . . ."

"We're taking a jitney to Colored Town!" Laura said.

"We're *in* Colored Town," Patsy said flatly.

"Are we, Grandma? Laura asked.

"W-w-what's C-colored Town?" Jean asked.

May answered them both, "Yes, we're in Colored Town. And it's where all of the colored people in town live."

"Everyone colored?" Laura asked. "How do they all fit?"

"I wanna go to Colored Town!" Annie May added.

"Clarksville is bigger than you think, child," the grandmother answered. "The colored churches and businesses, the colored school— all in Colored Town."

"And it's a good-sized school now, too. Not the one-room schoolhouse I taught in all those years ago," May added. "Glad to see they're doing more for the colored citizens here in Clarksville."

"Can I stay with you, Grandma, while they go visiting?" Patsy asked softly.

"If your mother says it's all right," she answered.

"Mama?" Patsy asked.

"Sure, I don't see why not . . ."

"You know, May, you were Patsy's age when you learned how to quilt. Maybe this would be a good time for me to give this girl her first quilting lesson. Would you like that, Patsy?"

Patsy nodded. Grandma Jackson leaned over and kissed her on the forehead. "Now let me get that jitney."

༄

"Your first quilt doesn't have to be very big. This one will be what you call a lap quilt." Grandma Jackson spoke as they sat at the dining room table, cutting fabric into strips one and one-half inches wide by six and one-half inches long. Patsy used a pattern at first to get the strips the right size, but then she was able to cut by sight like her grandmother.

Grandma Jackson explained, "We'll cut these strips now, but when you get home, you can ask your mother for more fabric and add more strips of your own. I know your mother has taught you to sew . . ."

Patsy nodded her head. "I make clothes for my dolls. I made a dress for Annie May's doll before we left on this trip."

Her grandmother explained how to use the same small running stitches to sew the strips of fabric together in sets of six to make a quilt pattern called the Fence Rail. Watching Grandma Jackson sew the strips together, Patsy realized for the first time that they were both left-handed. She gave Patsy a brass thimble to put on the top of her middle finger. She showed her how to use the thimble to push the needle in

and out of the fabric. Patsy learned quickly and
worked silently.

"This is a nice, easy pattern for you to get
started with. As you finish your blocks of strips,
lay them out so that you can sew them together
with the strips of one block going up and down
like the posts in a fence, the next one sideways
like the rails. That's all there is to it. It'll look
a lot like a real fence when you're done—only
prettier!" the grandmother said, smiling at the
girl. "When the top is as big as you want, ask
your mother to give you a big piece of cloth for
the back. You'll need to cut an old blanket or
something for the batting in the middle. Use the
same running stitch I just showed you and sew
all three layers together. Then you'll take some
long strips of fabric to sew a binding around all
four sides and that's it—you'll have yourself a
nice quilt!"

Patsy paused and looked up from her sewing.

"You know," Grandma Jackson added, leaning
back in her chair and looking off past Patsy,
"I love to quilt. It helps take your mind off
whatever's bothering you. You can just set your
mind on making something beautiful. And when

you're doing that, nothing else seems to matter . . ." She took Patsy's hands in hers and looked her straight in the eyes. "I know that part of this trip wasn't very nice for you. I know it's hard for you to understand some parts of how we live down here . . ."

Tears started welling up in Patsy's eyes. "The conductor was mean to us, Grandma. And the colored car was dirty and it smelled so bad . . . there were ladies on the colored car who said mean things to Mama . . . the dress Mama made me got all dirty . . ."

Her grandmother continued, "But I want you to do this. Promise me you'll do this: With each stitch you make on this quilt, I want you to just let loose a bit of the pain you're feeling right now. The memories—just let them go. And when you finish, I promise you—as God is my judge, you have my word—you won't feel the hurt and ugliness and everything else about that old colored car. It will all be gone from your mind. More important, it will all be gone from your heart."

"Thank you, Grandma," Patsy said, wiping her eyes, "but I don't see how—"

"The more you quilt, the easier it will be to let the hurt go," Grandma Jackson said.

"I don't know, Grandma," Patsy said, shaking her head.

"One stitch at a time, child, that's how it works its way out of your heart . . . all of those bad feelings."

"You make it sound like it's so easy," the girl said.

"No, not easy. Just one stitch at a time," her grandmother said.

The two of them were silent for a long moment.

Then Patsy said, "I'll try, Grandma. I promise, I really will try."

Patsy and her grandmother sewed the rest of the afternoon and into the evening. They made several Fence Rail squares. They moved over to the quilting frame and worked on a quilt her grandmother had already started. She let Patsy practice sewing the three layers together, making the same small running stitch she used when she made her doll clothes, always moving the needle with the thimble, pushing firmly to get the needle down and up through the three thick layers.

"You're as smart with the needle as your mother," Grandma Jackson said.

Patsy smiled.

༄

Sunday was a day of visitors. Word spread that May Ford and her daughters were in town. Folks came by all afternoon and into the evening. Grandma Jackson brought all of the visitors to the back yard to sit in the shade. Patsy sat under the big tree and sewed on her quilt pieces. Laura, Jean, and Annie May played tag around the tree. When they got too hot and tired, they sat under the tree with Patsy and played jacks while she sewed.

May Ford put the girls to bed early, not long after sundown.

Around midnight, there was a scream coming out of the guestroom. It was Patsy. "Get your hands off of me! Get your hands off of me!" she cried out. "Mama, Mama," she screamed. May and her mother, pushing the door open so hard that it chipped the paint off of the wall behind it, rushed inside the room.

Patsy was awake then, sitting on the side of the bed, crying hysterically. Annie May, startled out of her sleep, was wailing. Jean and Laura, sound sleepers, did not wake up at all. Grandma Jackson wrapped her arms around Patsy while May held Annie in her arms and took her out of the room.

"Oh, Grandma! How do you live here? Everything is about colored and white down here—the colored car, the colored drinking fountain, the taxi driver wouldn't let us in his taxi because we're colored. Colored, white. Colored, white! Don't you get tired of it?" Patsy spoke between spasms of tears.

"'Course I get tired of it. 'Course I do, child," her grandmother said, still holding her tightly. "But this is my home. This is how we live right now. This is how we've always lived. Things will change, but not anytime soon. Not anytime soon, baby." The grandmother now held Patsy's face between her hands and steadied her gaze into the girl's eyes.

"You have a different home. A different

life. Things will be different for you—they *are* different for you. Now relax, dear. The bad part is over. It's all a dream. Now, go back to sleep . . ."

ᔕ

It was Wednesday morning. The train back home was scheduled to leave the Clarksville station at eleven o'clock that morning. Their three suitcases were evenly lined up just to the side of the front door.

"I don't want to go home if we have to get back on the colored car. I want to stay here with Grandma," Patsy said to her mother as they sat in two of the wicker chairs on the front porch. Patsy was steadily moving the needle in and out of the fabric as she sewed strips of the pattern together, eyes glued to the fabric as she spoke.

"There's no way around it, Patsy. That's part of the trip home," May Ford said.

Patsy was silent. She tensed up. She dropped her thimble and pricked her finger with the tip of the needle. A large drop of blood dripped onto the fabric.

"Ah!" she gasped as she saw the bloodstain on the cloth.

"Now I know that colored car wasn't very clean. But we'll be on and off the next one before you know it. "

"But I like being here with Grandma," Patsy said.

"I know you do, baby. We all do. And we'll be back to visit, sure enough," her mother said. "But you can't stay here. This isn't our world, and this isn't our life. And I think you know that—"

"Mama, please! I just don't want to get back on that colored car!"

Grandma Jackson came outside, followed by Laura, Jean, and Annie May. "All right, now. Don't these girls look as pretty as can be?" she said looking over at May and Patsy. All four girls were dressed in the same travel clothes they'd worn on the ride down to Clarksville. "Are you sure you won't stay a few days more?" she asked May.

"Mama, you know we've got to get back. I've got all that canning waiting for me," May answered.

"You work too hard!"

"No harder than you. I learned it all from you," she said, smiling.

Grandma Jackson turned to the girls. "Give me one more hug, everybody now."

The three youngest girls lined up in front of their grandmother.

"I don't know when I'll see these babies again," she said, hugging each one long and hard.

Patsy watched from her seat in the wicker chair. She could not tell if that was sweat dripping down her grandmother's cheeks or tears. She picked up her thimble and stuffed her sewing into the canvas bag Grandma Jackson had given her to hold her quilt pieces.

"Patsy!" the grandmother called out.

Patsy slowly got up and walked over to her grandmother.

"I want to see that quilt the next time I come up to Detroit to visit," Grandma Jackson said.

"I'll finish, Grandma, I promise."

"I know you will, child, I know you will. And remember what you do with each stitch of the quilt."

They hugged each other tightly. "I'll remember, Grandma," Patsy said softly.

"Let's get these suitcases on the sidewalk," May said. "The jitney will be here any minute, and we've got a train to catch!"

6

A Thousand Jars

"Mama, these grapes don't smell good. They smell funny," Laura said as she struggled to hold the long broom handle, sweeping around the bushel of purple grapes her father had placed near the door to the summer kitchen.

It was the last week in July—May Ford and the girls were home from Clarksville. They'd arrived at the Michigan Central Station late Thursday afternoon, and by Friday morning May was back in the summer kitchen.

May stood at the stove, another bushel of grapes and a bucket of water at her feet, a large pot of water boiling on the wood-burning stove. She had spent the morning taking one bunch of grapes at a time from the bushel, washing them off in the pail of water, and then putting them— stems and all—in the boiling water. These were the first steps to making grape jelly. "It's the heat," she said, stopping to wipe the sweat off her forehead with her apron. "The grapes are ripe and the heat makes the smell seem stronger, that's all. These are good grapes. Your father got these bushels from the cherry man this morning."

Patsy was sitting on the bench on the other side of the door, sewing more fabric strip pieces together. She had been sewing practically nonstop since she left her grandmother's house and got on the train. She stepped up into the train—the colored car—from the platform of the Clarksville train station, sat in her seat by the window, and never looked up. Not once. She did not speak. She kept her eye on her fabric and focused on her needle, rocking gently with the movement of the train as she sewed. Her sisters played and chattered among themselves. Her mother offered her one of the peaches a neighbor had brought by as they were packing up the jitney. "No thank you, Mama," she said and kept to her quilt. She did not look up until the conductor entered the train and announced, "Next stop Cincinnati!" She looked up at her mother and smiled. May put her arm around her and kissed the top of her head.

Patsy looked up from her quilting when she heard her mother say "cherry man." Patsy had been calling that particular fruit and vegetable vendor the cherry man for as long as she could remember. Her mother and sisters picked up on the name and called him the same thing.

But even though the cherry man had an Italian name just like the other fruit and vegetable vendors, he was different: he drove a Model A pickup truck, just like Douglas Ford and his drivers. And her father said he sold the best fruit in town. The other evening at dinner, their first meal back home, her father said he and the cherry man might be making a business deal. The cherry man was going to buy a new truck. "He wants to sell me his old truck," their father said.

All of the peddlers that came down Halleck Street, cherry man included, knew by now that May Ford put away a thousand jars of food for her family each summer and they would need to keep coming with their produce, ripe to the day, in order to fill those jars. Patsy knew it, too. She counted one year: she took a pad of paper and her pencil and tallied up the jars in the cabinet in the back room and in the row of cabinets in the cellar. She made a mark for every ten jars she counted, and it added up to one thousand jars.

༄

The sound of Douglas Ford's donkey saw buzzed in the background. May sloshed the grapes in the water and then carefully dropped them in the boiling pot. She had already gone through one bushel of grapes and was working on the second. Jean and Annie May were fussing in the back room.

"Laura, go see about the girls," the mother said.

"Aww, Mama," Laura answered, leaning against the broom. "Why can't Patsy do it? And how come I have to sweep the floor and Patsy gets to sit around and sew all day long? Why don't you make her work, too?" Laura asked her mother.

"Do as I say, now," the mother said, still busy at the stove.

"But, Ma—"

"Hush! Goodness knows you've got a mouth on you. Now do as I say!"

Laura dragged her broom behind her as she went into the back room.

The night May and the girls got home, Patsy told her mother what Grandma Jackson had said to her when they first sat down to quilt. "Mama, Grandma said for me to keep sewing on the quilt. And each time I make a stitch for me to let loose some of the bad feelings from the colored car and the mean conductor . . . She said by the time I finish the quilt, the thoughts and memories will be gone from my mind, Mama. She said I won't feel bad about it . . ."

"Bless your heart," May said to her. "Well, your grandmother has made many a quilt. And if she said that, then that's what you do."

"Mornin' May!"

Patsy looked up. It was Mrs. Chambers from next door, standing in the doorway.

"Mornin' Cleota," May answered.

As she stepped into the summer kitchen, Mrs. Chambers looked down at Patsy working her quilt and handed her a piece of bright-yellow cotton fabric. "Here's something from an old apron of mine," she said to Patsy.

"Thank you, ma'am," Patsy said, looking up but not quite making eye contact. Patsy did not know who her mother had told about the trip to Clarksville and the trouble on the colored car, but in the few days since their return, the other women from the neighborhood who often came by the house—Mrs. Chambers, Mrs. Carson, Mrs. Yablonski, even Mrs. Jones who lived one block behind on Burnside—seemed to know about the quilt and had already stopped by with a piece of fabric in hand for her to cut and piece into it.

"Looks like you need these buckets filled," Mrs. Chambers said as she bent over and reached for one, looking heavier than usual and already short of breath even before filling one bucket.

"Yes, Cleota, thank you kindly," May said standing over the pot and stirring the grapes.

"Look at those hands of yours, May!"

Patsy noticed, too. They were a deep purple color. The same color as the grapes.

"Can't be helped," her mother said. "You can't make grape jelly and not color your hands."

Patsy knew that, too. Even though she had never made the jelly herself, she had watched her mother often enough and knew the process by heart. It was messy now and would get even messier. After rinsing and boiling the grapes, stems and all, her mother let the mixture cool a bit and then strained it through a muslin bag over another large pot. She strained it over and over two or three times. "The more times you strain it, the clearer the jelly," her mother would say. Patsy knew it was true. She could see through a jar of her mother's jelly almost as if she were looking through a glass window.

Then her mother added sugar and pectin. The pectin did the same thing as the stems from the grapes, her mother explained—it helped the mixture congeal. May put the pot back over the heat and let it boil until the juice was thickened. When it cooled, she filled jars with the thick liquid. She sealed the jars with lids that she screwed on tight. Then she set those jars in boiling water—a bath was what she called it—

for five or so minutes. After that, the final step was to let them cool in a corner of the room.

"Save a jar or two for me," Mrs. Chambers said.

"You know I always do," May Ford said, straining the grape mixture through the muslin bag. "Glad to share it with you."

"You know, sometimes I think you'd feed the whole neighborhood if you could!" Mrs. Chambers said as she picked up a second bucket.

"Don't start now, Cleota." May answered. "You know I'm not going to let anyone go hungry if I can help it."

"Some folks don't want your help, if you know who I mean."

"You mean Mr. Williams? That man doesn't scare me," May said, shaking her head. "Anyway, I do it for the kids, not for him."

Patsy watched Mrs. Chambers go out and then return with the two buckets filled to the brim with water. "For the life of me, I don't see how you can work over that hot stove all day like that in this kind of weather. Makes me sweat just to look at you!" Mrs. Chambers said. Water sloshed onto the floor as she walked over to the table.

May Ford looked away from her pots and down at the floor. Mrs. Chambers looked over at her friend, but before May could say a word, she said, "Sorry about the mess, May, I'll get it right up."

Mrs. Chambers reached for the mop and started wiping the water up off the floor. While she worked, she asked, "Why's your husband at the saw this afternoon? Isn't he usually at the factories this time of day?"

"He and his drivers had extra loads of wood from the factories yesterday. He was up late last night at the saw—"

"I heard him," Mrs. Chambers interrupted, "way past dark."

"—and he's been at that saw all afternoon, finishing up before the deliveries," May answered, squeezing the juice through the muslin a second time.

Mrs. Chambers stepped closer to May and lowered her voice to a whisper. Instinctively, Patsy leaned forward, but she could not hear a thing coming out of the woman's mouth. But she did hear some of what her mother replied as she tried to whisper while she strained the jelly mixture: " . . . yes you heard right, it got ugly," " . . . no, I hadn't told her," " . . . my Lord, why is everybody trying to tell me how to raise my children? That's enough now, we'll talk later."

"No harm intended," Mrs. Chambers said in a normal tone of voice as she turned to leave. "I'm going to try to catch a little breeze out in the yard." Then, as she stooped to pick up the bushel of grapes by the door, she said, "Let me bring these grapes over to you. You're about ready for them—goodness gracious." She pulled her head back. "What's that smell?" She put the grapes down near the buckets over where May Ford stood at the stove.

May finished straining the rest of the grape liquid and then leaned way forward, putting her nose closer to the bushel basket. She began lifting bunches of grapes and putting them in the buckets of rinse water. Then she shrieked, "Good Lord, would you look at this!"

Patsy threw her quilting down on the bench and rushed over. Mrs. Chambers leaned over the basket and, shaking her head, said, "Have mercy!"

Patsy stood between the two women and saw what they saw: at the bottom of the basket was a large pile of moldy, rancid grapes. Instead of a bright purple color, they were covered with a black-and-white fungus. The grapes themselves were almost a brown color. The smell made Patsy feel sick to her stomach. She quickly stepped back, holding her hand up to her mouth.

"Douglas!" May Ford called out, running to the doorway. "Douglas!"

The whir of the saw stopped. Laura, Jean, and Annie May came running into the front room and ran straight to the bushel basket, peering in.

"Eee-yuck! Pee-yew!" the two younger girls screamed.

Annie May bent over deep into the bushel basket, "What's in there, Mama?"

Her mother stepped quickly over to the basket and pulled her back, "Goodness, don't fall in there, Annie!"

"Mama, I told you those grapes smelled

funny!" Laura said, holding her sleeve up to her nose.

"Douglas," May called again, this time from where she stood at the basket, "come in here right away—there's something you need to see!"

Douglas Ford strode into the summer kitchen as she spoke. He peered into the basket and shook his head. "That looks bad," he said. "But I'll take care of it," he said. "Giuseppe's coming by this evening to talk about selling that truck of his. I'll see to it then."

༺

The Ford family was seated around the kitchen table. They had just finished eating dinner.

"Dad, can I go out with you when you talk to him?" Doug Jr. asked.

"No, son," the father replied, "but you can go out there now and put that bushel of rotten grapes next to my saw."

"Yes, sir!" he said. Doug hurried out the back door.

It was usually Patsy who asked if the girls could be excused from the table. Laura looked at Patsy, waiting. Patsy turned in her seat and faced the kitchen window. Through the screen, she could see her brother dragging the basket and hear it scraping against the driveway.

"Mama," Laura asked, "may we leave the table?"

May Ford looked at each of their plates, all empty. "That's good, girls," she said, "go on, now."

Jean and Annie May followed Laura into the dining room. Jean stopped and turned to Patsy. "Patsy, do you want to play dolls with us?"

Patsy stared out the kitchen window.

"Answer your sister, Patsy," the mother commanded.

"Not now," she answered, still facing the window.

"Go on, girls," the mother said, standing by the sink. "Patsy, I'm not going to have you just sit there and ignore your sisters like that. It's all right to be quiet while you're sewing—"

Doug burst in through the back door. "The cherry man just pulled up!" he announced.

Their father left the kitchen without saying a word. Doug stood next to Patsy as they both peered out the kitchen window. May Ford

116

watched from where she stood at the sink.

The cherry man and their father shook hands.

"Come, Mr. Ford, I come by for you to look at the truck." He spoke with a thick Italian accent. "See, it's parked right over here."

"Giuseppe, I want you to see this bushel of grapes here," Douglas Ford said, interrupting and pointing to the basket.

Douglas walked with him over to the saw. He stood next to him as he peered down into the basket. The cherry man shook his head.

"Mr. Ford, I don't know what happened. You know I give you good produce for your wife." He scratched the back of his head.

"That last bushel of sweet peppers you gave me, looked like half the basket was spoiled as well. I picked them out before I gave the basket to my wife. I didn't say anything to you then because I figured it was a mistake. Now, it's starting to look like a pattern."

"Oh no, Mr. Ford! Mr. Ford, you know I bring you the best fruit in the city."

"That's what I like to think," Douglas said to him.

"I bring another bushel tomorrow morning.

117

Everything will be fine, I promise!" he said. "Promise. Now please, come look at the truck."

"Giuseppe, the deal's off with the truck," Douglas said.

Still watching from the kitchen window, Patsy gasped and put her hand up to her mouth. Doug leaned in closer to the window screen. "My goodness," May whispered, wiping her forehead with her apron.

"Oh, no, Mr. Ford. Please, I promise to bring you more grapes tomorrow."

"That's it, Giuseppe. The deal's off. If I can't depend on you to bring decent fruit for my family, I'm not going to take a chance on that truck of yours."

"I drive it every day. The truck is good. You have my word."

Douglas Ford picked up the bushel of grapes and handed the basket to the cherry man. "Take these with you," he said. He turned and walked toward the back door.

Doug and Patsy looked at their father as he walked into the kitchen. He sat down at the kitchen table. "May," he said turning to his wife, "I'd like a nice cool glass of lemonade."

Grandma Ford's Grape Jelly

Recipe courtesy of the Ford family archives

1. Wash grapes in plain water. DO NOT remove from stems. (This is Grandma Ford's unique direction: there is pectin in the stems.)
2. Put grapes in large pot. Cover grapes with water.
3. Over medium-high heat, bring to a rolling boil.
4. Set aside; cool.
5. Strain contents of pot through muslin bag 2 times at least. Stems, seeds, and skins will be caught in the bag as you strain the grape liquid. (The more you strain, the clearer the jelly.)
6. To 4 cups of grape juice, add 4 cups of sugar and 1 pouch of CERTO® fruit pectin.
7. Return juice to pot and bring to boil. Be sure not to have heat too high or juice will boil over. Watch the pot!
8. Let juice continue to boil until it passes "saucer test." (Put a teaspoonful of juice in a saucer and see if it congeals when cool.)
9. When it passes "saucer test," remove juice from heat. By now, it should have decreased in volume quite a bit.
10. Wash jars thoroughly and rinse thoroughly in very hot water. Keep jars warm until ready to fill.
11. Fill jars to within 1 inch from top.

continued on next page

12. Seal jars tightly with new warm lids.
13. Process in boiling water bath for 5 minutes.
14. Carefully remove jars from water. (Use a canning jar lifter.) Place on dry towel until cool.
15. Store in a cool place.

7

Twenty Squares

"I smelled the horse droppings this morning," May Ford said to her husband.

It was washday. May talked as she hung white sheets up to dry on the clothesline behind the house. Patsy stood close by holding a basket full of clothespins within arm's reach.

"I bought you a couple a bushels of peaches from that peddler fella," Douglas Ford said. "We're in the first week in August and he said this was prime time for fresh-picked peaches. His horse did his business while I was paying him."

"Mmm-hmm . . . Well, I just hope his peaches are as good as the ones from the cherry man," his wife said, taking a handful of clothespins from the basket and moving along the line. "Early August or not, his were always just right, good and sweet."

"May, what we've got will have to do. I don't think we'll be seeing much of the cherry man comin' down Halleck Street anymore."

"Shame," she said, shaking her head. Then, turning to her daughter, she said, "Come on, Patsy."

Patsy followed her mother into the house. The wringer washer was in the bathroom. On washdays, her father wheeled it in from the back porch. He filled the machine tub with pots of hot water heated on the wood-burning stove in the kitchen. May Ford's was the only wringer washer in the neighborhood. When it first arrived, Patsy noticed the neighbor women showed up on washday. They stood around and talked while they watched the clothes go from the sudsy water in the machine tub, through the wringer, and finally into the rinse water in the bathtub. Then May Ford would swing the wringer around and put the clothes back through the wringer and back into the rinse tub. She did this two or three more times.

"Clothes don't look so clean if there's soap still left in them," she had explained to Patsy.

It was Patsy's job to catch the laundry when

it came out of the wringer, after that final rinse, and put it in the laundry basket. She was doing just that on that particular workday when her mother turned to her and said, "Go check on the girls."

୨

Jean and Annie May were sitting at the kitchen table, playing with their dolls. Laura was leaning on the kitchen windowsill talking through the screen to someone. Patsy sat at the table, stitching together the Nine Rail patches that would form the top of the quilt. She sewed and listened. It was Laura's friend, Dottie Chambers from next door.

"Come on out, Laura, and play some hopscotch. I'm gonna do twenty squares!" Dottie announced.

"No you aren't," Laura said.

"Uh-huh!"

"Uh-uh!"

"You come on out here and see!" Dottie said. "And bring Jean and Patsy. I'm gonna get Janie and Maxine and maybe some other girls. My mother said for us to go down to the end of the block 'cause there won't be many folks walking by and we won't be in anybody's way. Then you'll all see. I'm gonna do twenty squares!"

Laura turned to Jean. "Did you hear that?" Jean was braiding her doll's hair. She looked up, smiled, and nodded.

"Hopscotch! I wanna play hopscotch," Annie May said.

And then Laura saw Patsy. "Patsy, take us down the street. Dottie says she's gonna do twenty squares. I don't think she can. *Nobody* does twenty squares!"

Patsy shrugged. She looked down at the fabric and kept sewing.

"Patsy, what's wrong with you? Don't you wanna see if Dottie's gonna do twenty squares?" Laura ran past Patsy and into the bathroom.

"Mama! Make Patsy stop sewing and take Jean and Annie and me down the block and play hopscotch. Dottie Chambers says she's gonna do twenty squares. I don't believe her. Nobody does twenty squares!"

"All right, then. Patsy, go on now with your sisters," their mother said from the bathroom. Patsy did not answer.

"Patsy? Put down your sewing now and go with your sisters," she said firmly.

"Yes, Mama," Patsy said, putting the fabric on the table.

"And you girls don't stop when you get to the Williamses' house. Walk on by. And when you get to Goddard, don't cross the street. Stay on this side of Goddard. Stay on this block," their mother said.

"Yes, Mama," both Patsy and Laura answered.

"Mama, c-c-c-an I see if Vochu wants to w-w-wants to c-c-ome, too?" Jean asked.

"Yes, go ask Mrs. Yablonski if Vochu can come with you," their mother answered. Then she called out to the baby, "Annie May, you come back here and sit with me. You can watch me while I do the wash."

"I don't wanna do wash. I wanna play hopscotch, too, Mama!" Annie protested. "Please?"

"Oh, all right. You can watch Dottie. But don't get in the way. And remember what I said now—stay on this block."

∽

When Jean, Vochu, Laura, Annie May, and
Patsy arrived down the block, the other girls
had already gathered to watch Dottie. Patsy's
friends were there: Janie Carson from across
the street and Maxine Allen from Burnside. The
two Williams girls were standing over to the
side, watching. Hazel was a little younger than
Jean. She held the hand of her sister, Nancy,
who was the same age as Annie May. Annie May
immediately went over and stood next to Nancy.
There were a couple of other girls there, too.
Patsy had seen them at school, but they were
older, in a higher grade, and she did not know
their names. Jean and Vochu kept to themselves,
giggling and whispering in each other's ears.
Vochu stood out as the only white face in the
bunch.

"Gimme room, now," Dottie said, holding
a small rock in her right hand and wiping the
sweat off of her forehead with the back of
her left hand. "I've gotta finish drawing these
squares!" The girls who were right next to her—
Janie and Maxine—stepped back.

Dottie leaned over close to the sidewalk and
put the rock to the concrete, holding it like a

stubby pencil. She had already drawn the first three squares of the grid, one on top of the other, and numbered them one, two, and three. They were each about a foot long and a foot wide. Next she drew squares four and five next to each other. Then square six standing alone, followed by seven and eight together. Nine, ten, and eleven stacked one above the other with twelve and thirteen together.

"Go on, Dottie!" The two older girls said.

Dottie stood up and smiled. She stepped back and looked at the squares so far. "Just seven more to go," she said, bending over again.

Square fourteen, then fifteen on top. Sixteen and seventeen together. Eighteen, nineteen, and twenty stacked to the finish. Dottie stood up and held the rock up in the air.

"It looks good, Dottie," Laura said, looking over at her friend.

"It sure d-d-does, D-d-d-dottie," Jean said.

The older girls looked at each other. "Why does she talk funny like that?" one of them asked.

"That's just how she talks," Janie said, not looking at either one of the two girls.

"I never heard anyone talk like that," one of the older girls said, then they both giggled.

Patsy looked over their way, then turned back to look at Dottie.

"Here I go!" Dottie announced.

Dottie threw the same rock she had used to make the hopscotch grid into the first square. Raising her left leg, she hopped with her right foot over square one and hopped into square two, hopped into square three, and then placed both feet down, one in square four and the other in square five. A hop into number six, one foot each in squares seven and eight. Hop nine, hop ten, hop eleven, and then she landed with both feet again, one in twelve, the other in thirteen. Right hop into fourteen, then fifteen. Both feet down in squares sixteen and seventeen. She ended the line with a hop into eighteen, nineteen, and twenty. The two older girls started clapping but someone shushed them.

Dottie, her face glistening with sweat, kept her eyes glued to the ground as she turned from the hop in square twenty and, staying on the same leg, started back down the grid. Each time she landed on both feet, she took a deep breath before hopping down the next single squares. When she reached square number two, she leaned over, sweat dripping onto the concrete. Still balancing on her right leg, Dottie picked up the rock that she had thrown in square one. She hopped into square one and then out just as quickly. She had finished.

Sweat was streaming down her face and down from her underarms. The girls gathered around Dottie and clapped. Laura gave her friend a hug. The Williams girls and Annie May jumped up and down and stepped in closer to the others.

"You did it!" the girls said, talking over each other.

"I told you I could do it!" Dottie said. "I told you!"

"D-d-d-Dottie d-d-did it!" It was one of the older girls imitating Jean.

There was sudden silence among the rest of the girls. Janie and Maxine turned and looked at Patsy and then down at Jean. Jean was looking up at Patsy, but Patsy did not say a word. She stared down at the grid. Vochu stepped closer to Jean. The older girl's friend laughed and broke the silence.

"So who wants to see me go up again?" Dottie asked, looking around at each of the girls.

"I do!" Laura answered.

"Me too! Yes, do it, Dottie!" Janie and Maxine both yelled out.

Dottie looked over at Annie May with the Williams girls. All three nodded vigorously and smiled. Vochu nodded along with them.

"I d-d-do!" Jean stammered.

"I d-d-d-do, I d-d-do," the older girls said, imitating Jean.

"Stop m-m-making fun of m-m-m . . ." Jean tried to finish her sentence.

"I'll say what I want to," one girl said.

Maxine looked over at Patsy and mouthed to her, "Say something."

Patsy turned her head.

"OK, now, everybody look! Here I go," Dottie said.

She threw the rock into square two. She hopped into square one, hopped over two into square three, then both feet into four and five . . .

"G-g-go Dottie, g-g-g-go!" the two girls chanted.

"Stop it now," Dottie told them, "you'll make me mess up!"

Hop into six. Both feet down in seven and eight.

"G-g-go Dottie, g-g-g-go!" they still taunted.

"T-t-t-that's not funny!" Jean said, her head jerking as she spoke, her body tensing up.

"Oh yeah? G-g-go Dottie, g-g-g-go!"

"Patsy!" Jean called to her sister.

Patsy's eyes were closed. The heat, the girls standing around watching, the mean tone of voice coming from those two older girls. She was back on the platform at the train station in Cincinnati. She heard the conductor's voice, "*Oh yes, but I will touch your daughter. And I will drag her onto that car if I have to . . . Now you take this little picka—*" Patsy covered her ears.

"D-d-d-Dottie, can you d-d-do it?" the girls continued to taunt.

Janie leaned over, pulled Patsy's hands away from her ears, and whispered to her, "Say something!"

"You think you're something, don't you! You and your old hopscotch!" the girls were leaning in close to Dottie.

Patsy closed her eyes tight. She was seated inside the colored car. Her blue organdy dress was covered with soot. She heard the women saying, "She raised those girls to think they're too good for the colored car . . . Bet they know different now, don't they."

"H-h-hop, Dottie, h-h-hop!" the girls kept at it.

Vochu whispered in Jean's ear, "Let's go." Jean nodded. She reached over and touched Patsy on the elbow. Patsy jerked around, hitting Jean in the eye.

"Ouch!" Jean cried.

Dottie kept moving as the older girls taunted her—hop into square eighteen.

"Oh! I'm sorry!" Patsy looked down at her sister, who had her hand over her eye.

Before Dottie could hop into nineteen, she lost her balance. Patsy looked over just as Dottie hopped several times outside the grid and then tumbled onto the concrete.

There was the sound of a loud gasp coming from Patsy and the other girls: Laura, Jean, Vochu, Annie May, Janie, Maxine, and the Williams girls as they stood there, jaws dropped open, looking down at Dottie on the ground.

Dottie glared at the two older girls. "Look what you made me do!" she yelled at them.

"We didn't make you do nothing!" one girl said. "And nobody cares about you and your old twenty squares! Nobody cares!" The girls turned and started off toward Burnside.

Jean rubbed her eye with one hand while Vochu took her other hand and held it.

"Patsy, you should've . . ." Janie started to say.

But Patsy had already stepped away from them. She called out to the two older girls as they crossed over to Burnside, "You girls are mean!" she said. And then in an even louder voice, "You're just mean!"

Then Patsy slumped down on the grass by the hopscotch grid. "Grandma was wrong!" she moaned quietly.

Janie, stepping closer to her, bent down and whispered, "What are you talking about?"

"Grandma was wrong. She said it would go away, but I still see it. I still hear it. It won't go away!"

8

The Petition

It was mid-morning, it was hot, and it was humid. May Ford was in the summer kitchen cutting up string beans. It had been one week since May finished canning peaches, and now she was putting up string beans.

Patsy sat at the quilt frame that had been placed just outside the door of the summer kitchen, under the slight shade from the overhang of the roof. The previous week, Patsy had finished sewing together all of the Fence Rail squares into one large piece of fabric. May Ford had tacked onto a quilt frame the three layers—Fence Rail pattern on top, old blanket in the middle, worn tablecloth on the bottom—that would be stitched together to make the finished quilt.

Even with the little bit of shade, Patsy's face was wet with sweat. She wiped the perspiration that dripped from her forehead with the back of her forearm before the drops of sweat could fall onto any of the Fence Rail strips. She could not help but smell the scent of her own body as she sewed. The baby powder she had dusted under her arms earlier that morning had long since stopped masking the odor.

In spite of the heat, and still using the same brass thimble on her left-hand middle finger that her grandmother had given her in Clarksville, Patsy worked at getting the needle down through the thickness of three layers of material. She pushed firmly while guiding the needle from the top of the quilt to the bottom, sometimes using her right hand underneath the quilt to keep the fabric taut as she aimed the needle back up again, careful not to prick one of her fingers with the sharp point. Down and up, over and over, she ran the thread through the fabric layers until several even rows of stitches ran perpendicular to the Fence Rail strips and she could see it was beginning to look like a finished quilt.

It was so hot and the air was so muggy that Laura, Jean, and Annie May just leaned against the big tree behind the house and held their dolls, doing nothing with them in particular. Occasionally Patsy heard one of them mumble something about a doll named Sister and another reply something about a doll named Sister. But each of them had named their doll Sister—beginning with Patsy—so it was hard for her to tell whose doll was supposed to be doing what.

Early that morning, Patsy heard her mother talking to herself and saying out loud, "I don't expect to have any visitors today, that's for sure. Not in this heat . . ." And in fact, no neighbor women—not Mrs. Yablonski, nor Mrs. Chambers, nor Mrs. Carson—came by to visit May Ford as she washed and cut up a bushel of string beans in the stifling heat of the summer kitchen. No one came by to fill the empty buckets of water lined up under the table or just sit on the bench by the door and fan themselves while they talked about the heat. From where Patsy sat in front of the quilt frame, she could hear as her mother moved back and forth from the stove to the worktable. She leaned over to her right and looked into the front room. She locked eyes with her mother, who was carrying a huge pot from the stove over to the table.

Her mother grunted from the weight of the pot as she set it down.

"You can come in here and help me if you'd like." May held out a ladle toward her daughter with one hand as she used her apron to wipe the sweat from her face with the other hand. "I've already filled these jars with string beans. Use this ladle to scoop enough hot water from the pot to fill each jar up to about one inch from the top."

The girl was silent. "Patsy?" her mother asked.

"No thank you, Mama," Patsy answered as she settled back in front of the frame and continued quilting.

May worked alone that morning.

༄

Not yet noon, Patsy heard the sound of a truck engine. She looked up from her needle to see her father pull up into the driveway in one of his Model A Ford pickup trucks, her brother, Doug, in the seat beside him. They both jumped out as soon as their father turned off the engine. Their shirts were covered in sweat all across their sleeves, their chest, and back. But neither one of them seemed to mind. Without breaking his stride, Douglas Ford went straight to his donkey saw and started up that engine. Her brother went over to the back of the truck and began unloading the wood they had broken down that morning from the empty crates at the auto factories, stacking it in a neat pile next to his dad.

"Slow down, Doug," Patsy heard their father say. "Take your time unloading that wood. It's a hot morning. Take your time."

The sound of the *hee-haw hee-haw* whir of the blade cutting into the wood slats broke through the still, heavy air of the late morning. Their father stood at the donkey saw, the brim of his cap pulled down to shield his face from the sun, and methodically pushed the tray holding the wood into the blade of the saw. It did not seem to Patsy that he worked any slower because of the heat. Neither did she, as she sat at the quilt frame, still pushing her needle.

Above the din of the saw, she heard the sound

of another engine turning onto Halleck Street. It was too early for any of her father's drivers to return from their runs to the factories. Instead, she expected to hear the cherry man calling out, "Fresh fruits! I've got fresh fruits!"

But it was a different truck and a different man—a colored man, not Italian like the cherry man—announcing a delivery. "Iceman!" He said after stopping his truck in front of their driveway. "Ice here!"

The girls under the tree, all three at once, shrieked, "Ice!"

"Mama, can we have some chips of ice? Just a little ice?" Laura asked.

"M-m-mama, it's so hot!" Jean said.

"I want ice for my dolly. She's hot, too," Annie added.

"I'll make a nice pitcher of ice-cold lemonade when I stop to make some sandwiches for lunch," May Ford answered.

"We don't want to wait for lunch. It's so hot," Laura said, pouting.

"Hush, now. Don't whine and get yourselves all worked up," their mother said. The girls went quiet.

The iceman nodded at Douglas Ford, at his saw, as he walked toward the back of the house, using a huge set of tongs to carry a twenty-five-pound block of ice wrapped in a muslin cloth. "Ice here!" he said as he walked up the steps to the back porch.

The icebox was located on the back porch, just outside the doorway to the kitchen. It had two doors with long metal latches. The iceman pulled those handles down to open up the doors and placed the block of ice on a metal tray on the right side of the box. Even with the large block of ice taking up half of the space, it was still large enough that May Ford stored bottles of milk, leftovers from dinner, even meat when she purchased enough for a couple of days worth of meals.

"Mr. Ford," the iceman said as he stopped in front of the donkey saw on his way back to his truck. "Folks say you're looking to buy another truck."

Douglas Ford pulled the tray back and stepped away from the whirring blade. He pulled a handkerchief from his hip pocket and wiped his face. "I am," he answered. "What've you got?"

"I'm looking to sell my delivery truck over there and buy a bigger one. I'll give you a fair price."

Douglas looked over toward the truck. "I like what I see, but honestly it's just not big enough to carry my heavy loads of wood from the factories."

"Give it a closer look," the iceman suggested as he walked down the driveway. Douglas followed him out to the street. He walked to the back of the truck.

"It's a mighty fine truck. I can tell you've taken good care of it, but the bed's just too small. I can't use it," Douglas said.

The iceman walked over to the hood. "Take a look at the engine . . ."

Douglas Ford shook his head. "Sorry," he said. He touched the brim of his cap and turned back to his saw.

෨

May Ford was in the house making sandwiches. Patsy sat at the quilt frame. She had completed stitching over a quarter of the quilt stretched across the frame. She ran her hand on top of the finished portion, feeling the raised material between the lines of stitching. "I'll be done in no time," she said to no one in particular. She had inserted the needle to begin another row of running stitches when she saw it—a dark smudge near the top edge of the fabric. She put down her needle and tried to rub it out with the pads of her fingers, but that only spread it out across more of the pieced strips of fabric and made it look worse. Patsy knew how the smudge got there: it was soot from the train ride home. It was soot from the ride home in the colored car. That train car had been just as dirty as the first one going down to Clarksville.

She spit into her fingers and used them to rub against the fabric. She rubbed harder, but the stain only looked darker. "Mama!" she called. She wanted her mother to look at the stain. She raised her voice. "Mama! Can you help me get this dirt out of my quilt?"

"What's that, Patsy?" her mother asked. "I can't make out what you're saying. Let me finish these sandwiches first . . ."

Patsy kept rubbing. Then Pointo, their hound dog, started barking. Her father turned off the saw. Still working to get out the soot, Patsy looked over in his direction. Her brother was sitting on the ground near the pile of wood he had stacked by the donkey saw, intently picking splinters out of his fingers.

It was Mr. Yablonski, their next-door neighbor, walking up the driveway. He walked over to the saw. He and Douglas Ford shook hands. Mr. Yablonski, leaning in close, whispered something to him. Her father creased his brow and, looking over to the summer kitchen, called out, "May!"

"I'm in the house making lunch," May Ford said from the inside kitchen.

Their father led Mr. Yablonski into the house through the back door. Patsy had never seen him enter their house before. She looked at the girls under the tree. "Somethin' bad just happened," she said to her sisters in a low voice.

Patsy got up from the quilt frame and crossed the yard over to the back door. She pressed her left ear against the screen.

"Oooh, I'm a t—," Laura almost finished her

sentence, but Patsy turned to her sister and raised a finger to her mouth. Laura stopped her threat, put down her doll, and ran up the back steps next to where Patsy stood.

Their neighbor was no longer whispering. Like his wife, Mr. Yablonski spoke with a heavy Polish accent.

"Meester Ford," Mr. Yablonski said, "I want to tell you that I deed not sign. I would never sign such a thing. You are a good neighbor. I deed not have good neighbors like you even back in the old country."

"Tell me what's happened," Douglas Ford said calmly.

"It's what you call a pe-tee-tion, I think they said. I looked at it. I saw the names, but I would never sign such a paper."

"What is this petition about?" Douglas asked.

"It's about the noise. Your saw, cutting the wood in the morning, in the night . . ." his voice trailed off.

"Goodness Lord!" May Ford said.

"Anything else on it?" Douglas asked.

"They want to take you to court. They want a

judge to tell you to stop the noise with the saw," their neighbor answered.

"Oh Douglas, who would do this to us? And what does this mean for our business? All these years we've worked so hard!" May said. Her voice was starting to quiver.

"Whose names are on the petition?" Douglas asked the neighbor.

"You know them all," he answered.

"Tell me. Please," Douglas asked again.

"I did not sign. I tell my Eva, we will not sign that paper."

"Please, who signed the petition?"

"I would never sign such a paper, Mr. Ford. Never." Then he began listing the names, "Carson, Chambers—"

"No wonder Sadie and Cleota didn't stop by this morning. I thought it was because of the heat!" May interrupted.

"May, let him finish," Douglas said.

"Harold Williams, his wife, Gustaf and Luba Meinhof, Kowalski, Johnson . . ."

"Your driver Johnson?" May asked.

"Lord, I hope not!"

Mr. Yablonski continued, "Joseph Smith, his

wife Gertrude, there were so many names, Mr. Ford, I cannot remember them all. But it was the neighbors, Mr. Ford. Our neighbors. You know them all."

There was silence.

Then Douglas Ford said. "Thank you, Mr. Yablonski . . ."

"Yes, thank you and Eva," May added.

"You're a good neighbor and a good friend," Douglas said.

Patsy almost pushed Laura down the steps as she turned to get back to her quilt frame. "Sorry," she whispered.

Laura moved quickly, as well, and ran back over to the tree. Patsy sat down at her quilt just as Mr. Yablonski opened the back door. He pulled a handkerchief out of his pocket and wiped the sweat off of his face. He walked past the Ford children without saying a word.

The parents remained in the house and continued their talk. It was harder to make out what they were saying from where Patsy sat, but she heard this much.

"Douglas, how could they turn on us like that? Our friends? Our neighbors. They knock on our door to use our telephone. We've never turned any of them away when they couldn't pay for wood to heat their homes."

The father answered, "I'll get to the bottom of this. Someone's behind all this. I'll find out who it is, and he'll have to answer for it."

9

The Summons

"It's a summons," Douglas announced to May Ford as he entered the summer kitchen. Then he asked, "What you got there?"

"Okra, hot peppers. What are you talking about?" May asked. "What is this?"

Douglas Ford had been cutting wood at the donkey saw all morning long. Patsy caught the scent of sawdust on his clothes as he strode past her, brushing up against the back of the chair where she sat at the quilt frame working her needle. He walked so quickly that she barely saw him, but she did see out of the corner of her eye that he held a sheet of paper in his hand.

"The mailman just delivered it—a registered letter, postmarked August 12. I had to sign for it," he said.

Patsy put down her needle and thimble, got

up, and stood in the doorway. Neither one of her
parents seemed to notice her standing there.

"Well, what is it?" her mother asked. She was
filling jars of okra mixed with hot red pepper
pods with steamy, boiling water.

Her father started reading from the paper,
"The Court of the Common Pleas for the City
of Detroit in the State of Michigan, Plaintiffs
Harold Williams, et al., versus Defendant
Douglas Ford Sr. The Defendant is hereby
ordered to appear before this court at 9 o'clock
in the morning on Monday, the 23rd day of
August, in the year of our Lord 1937. The
Defendant is hereby ordered to answer the
complaint of nuisance to the neighborhood
for the noise caused by the same Defendant
by the running of his saw during the day and
during nighttime hours as well. The Defendant
is summoned to appear before this court and
to answer the charges of this complaint. Herein
ends the complaint."

"So there it is, Williams versus Ford," her
father said, folding the summons and putting
it in his back pocket. "Harold's name is on the
complaint. That means he filed it. But I gotta

believe someone put him up to this. He doesn't have the brains to think of this himself!"

"Doesn't take brains to be mean," her mother said, shaking her head. "It's not too much noise when they knock on our door because they need wood in their stoves to stay warm in the middle of winter. Goodness knows, Douglas . . ."

"Now May, don't get yourself all riled up," her father said.

"How can you say that?" she asked. "They call themselves our friends? What kind of friends sign a petition so they can take you to court? Answer me that, Douglas!" She poured boiling water into one more jar of okra and peppers.

"You notice not one of the others has come by here since word of that petition got around," she added. "Eva—God bless her for not getting mixed up in any of this—Eva Yablonski came by yesterday and stayed for a while. She filled some buckets for me. But not one of them who signed that petition . . ."

"May, let me help you here." Douglas Ford bent over and picked up one of the empty buckets from under the worktable. "I'll fill this for you," he said.

As he stood up, he bumped up against the table. The table shook, knocking over two of the jars. Boiling hot water spilled onto May Ford's right hand as she tried to steady the table.

"*Aaagh*—good Lord!" May yelled out, pulling her hand away.

"Oh, May, I'm sorry!" Douglas said.

May quickly wrapped her hand in her apron and held it up to her chest.

"Let me look at it," he said.

"No, I'm fine . . ."

"Let me see it!"

May unwrapped her hand. It was red from the scalding water.

"God, this hurts," she said. "Good thing I'm left-handed . . ."

"I'll get some water in this bucket and put some ice in it. You need to soak that hand in ice water," he said, moving fast.

Patsy had stepped away from the doorway just after the water spilled and was back seated at the quilt frame, needle in hand.

"Patsy, go get another bucket and bring it over to the faucet," her father said, looking over at his daughter on his way over to the faucet.

151

Patsy did not move.

"Do as I say, *now*!" her father ordered.

"Yes, Daddy," she said as she hastily got up, stepped into the summer kitchen, and did as she was told.

10

Piano Lessons

"I'm finished, Mama," Laura announced to her
mother, getting up from the bench in front of
the upright piano in the living room. May Ford
stood in the kitchen doorway, cradling her
right hand—still red from the scalding that
morning—in the palm of her other hand.

"Laura, I hardly call that practicing," their
mother said. "You played a C scale maybe two
times . . ."

"But I was playing both hands together,"
Laura protested.

"Hush now, now sit back down and—" But
before May Ford could finish her sentence, Jean
had taken her sister's place on the piano bench
and was hammering out a C scale.

"See, M-m-m-mama, I c-c-can play my C scale,
too!" Jean said proudly.

"That's good," their mother said, "that's very nice."

Patsy sat at the dining room table, holding Annie May in her lap. May looked over at the two girls. "Patsy, piano lessons today. You and your sisters go see Mrs. Lewis for your lessons. I talked to her last Sunday at church. She's expecting you this afternoon."

"But, Mama, I haven't been practicing . . . I've been working on my quilt," Patsy said.

"No matter," their mother said, "Mrs. Lewis knows we've been out of town. Anyway, it's been three weeks now since we've been home. Time to get back to your lessons."

May reached into her apron pocket and with her left hand pulled out a one-dollar bill. She walked over to where Patsy sat. Patsy caught the scent of their mother's perfume as she handed her the money. Annie May reached over and grabbed their mother's right hand. May winced.

"You hurt your hand, Mama?" Annie May said.

"I hurt it this morning, working in the summer kitchen." Then she said to Patsy, "This dollar is for Mrs. Lewis . . ."

"I wanna piano lesson, too," Annie May said.

"We'll have a lesson, just the two of us, after the girls leave."

Annie May jumped off of Patsy's lap, ran into the living room, and climbed onto the piano bench.

"Now gather up your music books, all of you. It's about time for you girls to get going. And watch the clock. Finish up so you'll be home before evening sets in."

～

Mrs. Lewis held open the screen door. "Welcome, please come on in," she greeted her students. She led them into the parlor, which was sparsely furnished. There was a bench in front of a grand piano, a chair to the left of the bench where Mrs. Lewis sat, and a plush, maroon velvet sofa against the wall where the students waited their turn to play. Patsy noticed that Mrs. Lewis was wearing the same perfume as her mother.

As the three Ford sisters entered Mrs. Lewis's parlor, Laura announced, "I practiced my lessons, Jean and Patsy haven't."

Patsy remained silent. But Jean turned to Mrs. Lewis and said, "Yes, I d-d-did! I p-p-practiced." Her body tensed, her head twitched to one side as she spoke.

"Jean, I'm sure you did. You always come to your lessons prepared and ready to make music," their teacher said. "In fact, let's begin with you this afternoon."

Mrs. Lewis walked over to her seat by the piano and sat down.

"But Mrs. Lewis!" Laura said, pouting.

She did not say a word in response to Laura's outburst. She just nodded at Patsy and Laura; they knew to go sit and wait their turn on the sofa.

To Jean, who was now sitting on the bench, she said, "Let's warm up those fingers by playing some major scales. Let's start with the C scale."

Jean played the C scale. She even remembered to play the b-flat in the F-major scale. She struggled a bit through a Bach minuet, losing her place as she tried to read the notes, but Mrs. Lewis praised her just the same.

"Bravo, Jean! You're coming along so nicely."

She wrote practice instructions in the girl's notebook for the coming week.

When Mrs. Lewis called for Laura, the two sisters switched seats.

"So, Laura my dear, show me what you've been practicing this week," Mrs. Lewis said to her.

Laura moved her fingers quickly over the piano keys, playing her scales with chords and cadences. She played a different Bach minuet than the one in Jean's lesson. Her last piece was the spiritual "My Lord What a Morning."

Mrs. Lewis helped her work out some parts of the song where she stumbled over the fingering.

"Laura, very nice lesson today," she said. "Continue on these same pieces. They're coming along beautifully."

Mrs. Lewis nodded at Patsy, who switched places with Laura.

"So, dear child," she said to Patsy, "have you been practicing your piano lessons?"

Patsy hesitated, then she answered, slouching and looking down at the keyboard, "No I haven't, Mrs. Lewis."

The teacher touched her back lightly. "Sit up

straight, my dear," she said. Patsy straightened her back.

"So what have you been doing to fill your time?" she asked.

"I've been sewing. My grandmother taught me how to make a quilt when we were in Clarksville last month. We were gone a week in the middle of July. I'm making a lap quilt. I've been working on it every day, and I'm almost finished with it." The girl's voice perked up as she spoke.

"Well, that's quick work," Mrs. Lewis said. "But then, you're a very smart young lady. I'm not surprised you took to the needle like you've taken to the piano."

She narrowed her gaze toward the girl and lowered her voice. "Don't neglect your lessons. You've been coming along so nicely. And before you know it, it will be time for you to play for the Sunday school classes at church when they start up again this fall. You want to be ready."

"Yes, ma'am," Patsy said softly.

Mrs. Lewis opened her arms wide and motioned to Jean and Laura. "Gather 'round, girls."

The two sisters hurried over and bumped into each other as they jockeyed for a position around Patsy on the bench.

"I've been doing some traveling myself this summer," she said, ignoring the small commotion between the sisters. She paused, then continued, "Have you heard of the concert singer Marian Anderson?"

Jean and Laura shrugged. Patsy nodded tentatively.

"My dear young ladies, the whole musical world has embraced her. She returned a year or two ago from a triumphant European tour. Maestro Toscanini, a world-famous orchestra conductor, said a voice like hers is heard only once in a century."

She paused again, this time looking each girl square in the eyes. "She's one of our own," their teacher added.

"She's colored?" Laura asked.

"Yes, my dear child, yes she is," their teacher answered proudly.

Then she leaned in closer to the sisters. "And I have something exciting to share with you young ladies . . ."

At that moment, Jean began jostling for a more secure position on the bench. She bumped into Patsy who, in turn, leaned into Laura, whose elbow slammed down hard on the bass end of the piano.

Mrs. Lewis gazed up to the ceiling and shook her head.

"Girls," the teacher continued, regaining her focus, "I experienced the honor of sitting in the audience of one of Miss Anderson's concerts!"

The sisters just stared at her, blankly. Laura rubbed her elbow.

"She had only a few months earlier returned from an acclaimed concert tour throughout Russia. And before she left for a series of engagements in South America—in fact she's probably down in Argentina right now—she made a stop in my hometown in Alabama."

"Did you hear her sing?" Laura asked.

"Why, yes," the teacher answered with an edge of excitement to her voice. "But first, a group of us, a rather large group at that, gathered at the train station to greet her upon her arrival. Can you imagine the excitement

when the train came to a stop and Miss
Anderson—"

"Was she riding in the colored car?" Patsy
asked, interrupting.

Mrs. Lewis paused and then answered, "Well
yes, this was in the South so she emerged from
the colored car. She stood on the platform—"

"Were her clothes . . . dirty?" Patsy
interrupted her teacher again.

"I believe she wore a dark suit so it was hard
to tell, but there was a bit of soot on the white
gloves she was wearing. I remember noticing
the streaks of dirt as she waved to the crowd
assembled on the platform—"

"She didn't *mind* riding in the colored car?"

"Dear child, Miss Anderson has sung before
royalty in Europe. She has performed before
adoring fans across this country. Riding in the
colored car is such a small part of her journey.
Such a small part."

"So she sang after she got off the train?" Patsy
asked.

"Yes, she sang later that evening."

"Was her voice—I mean, how did she sound?"

"Miss Anderson was in full voice and the

161

music was heavenly, absolutely heavenly. I am honored to be able to sit here and share my experience . . ."

Patsy glanced out the parlor window and saw that the afternoon sun was no longer shining. "Excuse me, Mrs. Lewis, but it looks like it's almost dusk out and we should be getting home now." Patsy abruptly stood up from the bench.

"Thank you for the lessons," Patsy said. She reached into her skirt pocket and handed over the dollar bill her mother had given her to pay for the lessons.

"Oh, girls, I hope I didn't keep you too long— but it does, indeed, look rather dark out there. Gather up your music and your notebooks. Your music is coming along nicely. Please be careful as you walk home."

She ushered the girls out of the parlor to the front door.

"Oh, I wish I had a telephone so I could call your mother and tell her you're on your way. But hurry along and do be careful!"

౿

As the girls stepped outside, Patsy could

see why it appeared so dark from the parlor window—heavy clouds hung low like huge, dirty cotton balls. A strong, fast wind blew the clouds across the sky: a summer storm was coming.

Mrs. Lewis lived on MacKay, just south of Davison. It would be a long walk home, several blocks, to Halleck Street. The girls walked the sidewalk three abreast as they hurried down MacKay Street, walking into the wind, clutching their music and notebooks tightly.

As they crossed Grant Street, Patsy heard a familiar engine coming up behind them. At first she thought it was their father, coming to give them a ride so they would be home before the storm. But as it got closer, she could tell it was not her father's truck. She turned her head and looked over her shoulder. She recognized the truck and the man inside. It was not her father, it was the cherry man. His Model A pickup truck barreled down MacKay. He was looking their way, and Patsy's eyes met his as he passed by.

"Is that the cherry m-m-man?" Jean asked.

"Yes, that was him," Patsy answered.

He turned the corner, going west toward Dequindre.

By the time the sisters reached that corner, Dearing Street, it had started raining.

"My music's getting all wet," Laura complained.

"It's not raining that hard," Patsy said. "But come on. Walk faster."

"It's g-g-g-getting d-d-d-darker," Jean stammered. "Are we almost home?"

"We will be. Come on now," Patsy urged the two of them.

They crossed Meade and the rain was coming down harder. They walked with their faces to the ground to keep the rain out of their eyes.

Patsy looked down at her music books. The pages were drenched and starting to curl. By the time they reached Cody Street, it looked almost dark as nighttime. And she heard a faint whistle.

"Wait," Patsy said. The girls stopped. "Listen. Do you hear that?" she asked.

"Hear w-w-what?" Jean asked.

"I hear it," Laura answered.

"Hear w-w-what?" Jean asked again.

"The whistle," Laura said.

"Somebody's whistling. I hear it louder now,"

Patsy said, lowering her voice.

"Who is it?" Laura asked.

"I don't know," Patsy answered.

"Are you scared?" Laura asked.

"No, I'm not scared. Why should I be scared?" Patsy said.

"I'm getting scared," Jean said.

"There's nothing to be afraid of," Patsy said.

"Then why did you stop?" Laura asked.

"Well, here, everybody give me your music," Patsy said. She put the stack of music under her left arm. "Now, let's hold hands."

They grabbed hands, Patsy holding Jean's left hand, Laura holding Jean's right. By the time they reached McLean, their clothes were soaked through and the whistle got louder.

"I'm all wet," Jean cried.

"Shhh! We'll dry off at home," Patsy said. "Halleck Street's just ahead."

"Is it the cherry man?" Laura asked.

"What?" Patsy asked.

"Is he whistling?"

"Why would he be whistling?"

"He just passed us back by Mrs. Lewis's place."

"So?"

"He's mad because Daddy wouldn't buy his truck."

"So?"

"Well just so!" Laura said. "Nobody else is out in the rain! It has to be the cherry man!"

"That's stupid!" Patsy answered.

"I hear him whistling," Laura said.

"It's d-d-dark and I'm scared!" Jean said.

"OK, stop." Patsy stopped. The girls stopped with her. They all listened. The whistle sounded close. Patsy's heart was beating fast and hard against her chest. She took a deep breath.

"Here's what we'll do," she said. "We're almost at Halleck Street. As soon as we get there, we'll turn the corner and we'll scream as loud as we can, and whoever's whistling will get scared when he hears us screaming and he'll turn and run away!"

"What if he doesn't run away?" Laura asked.

"He will," Patsy said. "He just has to. Let's go!"

Still holding hands, they rushed toward Halleck Street. Right before they reached the corner, they saw the form of a man turning the corner, and as if on signal, the three sisters stopped, closed their eyes tight, and screamed at the top of their lungs.

The man stopped; the whistling stopped.

Still screaming, Patsy peered out of her right eye, looking directly at the man.

"Doug!" she cried, opening the other eye as well.

Her sisters stopped screaming. They opened their eyes, too.

Their brother stood there, looking at them and shaking his head.

"What's the matter with you girls?" he asked.

Patsy stomped her foot and asked, "Why were you whistling?"

"Mama told me to whistle so you'd know I was coming. She said you might be afraid in the dark."

"We weren't scared," Laura said.

"Yes we w-w-w-ere!" Jean said.

Doug started to laugh.

"It's not funny!" Patsy said, raising her voice.

"Oh, come on now," their brother said. "I'm as wet as you all are. And Mama's waiting. Let's get on home." Doug turned back around the corner and the girls followed behind.

11

The Courtroom

The donkey saw was quiet that morning. Douglas Ford was not wearing work clothes and cutting wood outside in the wood yard. He was in the house, seated at the kitchen table, wearing his black suit and a black and gray striped tie. He smelled like shaving cream. He was finishing his last few spoons of oatmeal. The rest of the family was seated around the table, eating breakfast as well.

"Why are you wearing those clothes?" Laura asked after she shoved a spoonful of oatmeal into her mouth.

"I have some business to take care of downtown," their father answered.

"What kind of business?" Laura asked, still chewing.

"I have to go to court," he said. Then, looking

over at May, he asked, "Do you have that summons?"

"It's in my pocketbook," she answered.

Patsy remembered her father reading the summons in the summer kitchen—September 23. Their neighbors. The saw. Nuisance.

"Daddy, Mama, can I go with you?" Patsy asked her parents.

"What, child?" May Ford asked.

"*May* I go with you to the courthouse?" she corrected herself.

"Why, you're still in your pajamas. Plus I need you to watch the girls while we're gone."

"If she wants to come, let the child come along," their father said, pushing away from the table.

"Who's going to watch the girls?" May asked him as she left the kitchen.

"Doug will be here. He can take care of them just as well as anybody."

"Ah, Dad," Doug said, looking up from his bowl, "I told Frankie and Henry—"

"Well you'll just have to tell them you're busy this morning," their father said.

"Do you want to see m-m-my new d-d-doll?"

Jean turned and asked her brother. "Do you want to play d-d-dolls with me?"

"Play with my dolls too, Doug!" Annie said.

Doug put down his spoon and pushed back his bowl.

"Buck up now, son," the father said. "Keep an eye on your sisters while we're gone."

May called out to Patsy, "Put on the blue organdy dress."

"The blue dress?" Patsy asked. "But I wore that to Clarksville and back, on the train . . ."

"And you'll wear it today. Now hurry—your father and I are walking out right now." May Ford wore her navy-blue linen dress. She put on her short-brimmed straw hat and secured it with a small hatpin while she spoke. She picked up her purse and gloves and warned as she walked toward the back door, "If you aren't ready when your father pulls out the driveway . . ."

৩১

Douglas Ford pushed hard against the heavy oak doors and held them open as May Ford entered the courtroom. Patsy followed close behind. The room was filled with two columns of long wooden seats with straight backs. To Patsy, they looked like the pews at church, except in the courtroom, the backs were a little taller and straighter. The first person she saw was their next-door neighbor Mr. Yablonski, seated alone, over against the wall in a far corner of the room. He turned in their direction and nodded.

Seated in a large cluster a few rows over were men Patsy recognized from the neighborhood and who were friends of her father—Chambers, Carson, Smith, Meinhof, Kowalski. Those were the ones whose names she knew. There were others there that Patsy did not know, but she assumed they were there for the case against her father. They talked among themselves or looked straight ahead as she and her parents took their seats in the front of the courtroom.

The murmuring died down as a man in a brown uniform stepped to the front of the courtroom.

"Who's that?" Patsy asked her father.

"Shhh." Douglas Ford put his finger up to his lips. "That's the bailiff. He keeps order in the court," he answered in a whisper so low she could barely hear him.

Patsy jumped in her seat when the bailiff announced in a loud, booming voice, "Hear ye, hear ye, hear ye. The court of Judge Robert DiPonio is now in session. Please rise."

Patsy did what everyone else in the courtroom did—she stood up as the judge entered from a door at the back of the room. He walked up a few steps and took his seat behind a huge desk, raised so that he could look down on the courtroom below.

"Be seated," the bailiff instructed.

The bailiff walked up to the judge and they spoke in low tones. He then walked over to the clerk, who was seated at a small desk almost directly beneath the judge. The clerk handed him a sheet of paper. Reading from the paper, the bailiff announced, "The court calls the Plaintiffs Harold Williams, Walter Chambers, Luther Carson, George Kowalski, George Clark, Gustaf Meinhof, Robert Johnson, and Joseph Smith. Please step up to the bench."

Neighbors—colored and white—filed forward. They stood at the front of the room in the order in which they were called, beneath Judge DiPonio's desk. But where they all stood looked more like a rail than a bench. It was a thick heavy wooden railing that was waist high and where some of them rested their hands.

The bailiff then announced, "The court calls the Defendant Douglas Ford Sr. Please step up to the bench."

Douglas Ford got up from his seat, walked briskly to the front of the room, and stood next to his neighbors on the opposite end of the bench from where Harold Williams stood.

Next the bailiff said, "Please raise your right hands."

All the men standing raised their right hands.

"Do you swear to tell the truth, the whole truth, and nothing but the truth, so help you God?" he asked.

"I do," Douglas Ford and his neighbors answered.

The judge sifted through some papers, then looked down at the line of men standing below him. Clearing his throat he asked, "This is the Common Pleas Court, a small claims court. So there's no jury box. There's no witness box. The parties to this action will stand before me and we will proceed from here. You've all taken the oath. Who speaks for the Plaintiffs?"

There was a pause.

"I do," answered Mr. Williams.

"Please state your name and address for court," Judge DiPonio instructed him.

"Williams. Harold Williams. 2050 Halleck Street, Detroit, Michigan," he said. Then he added, "Your honor."

The judge continued, "Now according to this complaint, you and the other Plaintiffs have filed an accusation of nuisance against the Defendant. Please explain yourself."

"Well, your honor," Mr. Williams began, "Mr. Ford here has a wood business and wood yard right next to his house. And he cuts up that wood of his with this big saw. And he runs that saw all day every day, except Sunday that is. Sometimes he's out there early in the morning. Sometimes when we're trying to get to sleep, he's running that saw in the nighttime. You can hear it all up and down the neighborhood. So we got together a petition, and folks signed it saying we just want some peace and quiet."

"How long have you lived in your current residence?" Judge DiPonio asked Mr. Williams.

"Two years, sir," he answered.

"And these other gentlemen?" the judge asked of the other neighbors.

"Five years," Mr. Chambers answered.

"Eight years," Mr. Carson said.

"Ten years," Mr. Kowalski said.

"Four," Mr. Clark said in a low voice.

Mr. Meinhof answered, "Nine, your honor."

Mr. Johnson said, "Six, sir."

And Mr. Smith answered, "Three years."

The judge continued, "Mr. Williams, was Mr. Ford operating his business when you moved into your home?"

"Yes, your honor," he answered.

"And the rest of the Plaintiffs?"

"Yes," they answered in unison.

Judge DiPonio paused and looked down at his papers.

"And you, Mr. Ford, how do you answer the complaint?" the judge asked, shifting his focus.

"Your honor," Douglas Ford began, "I moved to Detroit from New Orleans, Louisiana, in 1922. I bought the lot at 1950 Halleck Street soon after I moved here. It's a double lot—one lot has my home, which I built, and the other lot has the wood yard. I started my business in 1923. I generally employ five drivers. Most of them live in the neighborhood. The drivers and I get scrap wood from the automobile factories. We bring it to my wood yard. That's where I have my saw. I cut it into pieces small enough to fit into wood-burning stoves, heating and cooking stoves."

Douglas looked over down at the row of his neighbors standing beside him. "Your honor," he continued, "I have always been on good terms with my neighbors. I hardly ever run my saw past dark in the warmer months. And not much past dark in the winter and fall. Sometimes if I or one of my drivers has brought in an especially large load of wood the night before, I run the saw early in the morning. But that doesn't happen too often."

He paused, still looking up at the judge. Judge DiPonio motioned with his head for him to continue.

"I know times are hard so I give my neighbors wood when they ask. I don't ask for any money. They pay when they can. Sometimes they do a little work for me to pay it off. I hire them full time if they can drive a truck when I need an extra driver for my business."

The judge looked down at Mr. Williams. "Have you received wood from Mr. Ford during the time you've lived in your current residence?" he asked.

"Yes, sir," Harold Williams answered, barely audible.

"Please speak up when you address the court," the bailiff said.

"Yes, your honor," Mr. Williams answered again, in a louder voice.

"And the rest of you?" the judge asked the other Plaintiffs.

"Yes."

"Yes, your honor."

"Yes."

Each of the other men answered as well, indicating that Douglas Ford had indeed provided wood for their homes and families.

"How many of you, at any time, have ever worked for his business?"

Chambers, Carson, Kowalski, Johnson,

Meinhof, Smith—their heads bowed slightly—
raised their hands.

Judge DiPonio read something on his desk,
then he continued, "Gentlemen, by your own
testimony, Mr. Ford was already operating
his business when each of you moved into
the neighborhood. In other words, he was
living in the neighborhood and running his
business, cutting wood with his saw, before any
of you moved there. You chose to move in and
therefore cannot complain about a condition that
was already existing. Furthermore," he leaned
forward as he spoke, "if Mr. Ford can't operate
his saw, he cannot run his business. And you
gentlemen—and I dare say many more of your
neighbors—have *all* benefited greatly from his
business. Mr. Ford has not only supported his
own family but has helped all of you care for and
support yours.

"Now the Common Pleas Court is a court
of equity. So while the noise from the saw,
according to the law, might indeed disturb the
peace of the neighborhood, considering all of
the facts of the case, the noise from the saw
and the wood business is mitigated by all of

the benefits Mr. Ford and his business have provided to you who are assembled here as well as the entire community."

Judge DiPonio hit his gavel hard against a large wooden block and declared, "I find no merit in the Plaintiffs' complaint of nuisance against the Defendant. Case dismissed!"

The judge stood up from his seat. May Ford let out a sigh of relief as she reached over and squeezed Patsy's hand.

"All rise!" the bailiff instructed.

The judge exited the courtroom.

The neighbors turned away from Douglas Ford as they left the rail. Douglas walked over to where May and Patsy stood smiling at him. He hugged them. Mr. Yablonski walked along the side aisle and greeted his next-door neighbor with a handshake.

"This is a good thing the judge did," Mr. Yablonski said.

"Yes, yes," Douglas said. "Thanks for coming." As Mr. Yablonski turned to leave, he added, "I really appreciate it, more than you know."

There was murmuring as the courtroom began to empty out. A few of the Plaintiffs, including Mr. Williams, went to their seats to retrieve their hats. He had to walk past Douglas Ford before he could leave the room.

"Harold," Douglas said.

Harold Williams looked startled and a little fearful. He glanced over at the bailiff.

"I'm not going to hurt you," Douglas assured him. "I got my justice here. I have no ax to grind with you. I just want to know, who put you up to this?"

"What are you talkin' about? What do you mean?" Harold asked.

"Aw, c'mon, Harold. Just tell me. Who got you to start the petition? File the nuisance complaint? Just tell me."

Harold looked down at the floor, fingering the rim of his hat. "It was that Italian fella. He drives the fruit truck. Gee, Geesu . . ."

"Giuseppe?" Douglas asked.

May Ford, who was standing nearby, gasped.

"Gee-gee-seppe," Harold stammered. "He said we shouldn't have to put up with that noise. He said it was a nuisance and the neighborhood would be better—"

Douglas held up the palm of his hand and cut

him off. He looked Harold straight in the eyes. "Did he pay you?"

There was silence.

"Yes," Harold whispered. He turned away and left the courtroom.

"Lord, have mercy," Douglas Ford said, shaking his head.

Patsy moved in closer to her father. "Daddy, the cherry man paid him to take you to court?"

"Yes, child," he answered.

"So, are you going to do anything about the cherry man?"

"Do anything? What's there to do? The case was thrown out of court. Whatever he wanted to happen didn't happen. You heard me tell Mr. Williams—I got justice. I just hope and pray this is the last of this mess."

He motioned for May and Patsy to join him as he headed toward the door.

12

Red Sky

It was late the next night and the house was quiet. In the bedroom off the kitchen shared by the three oldest sisters, Patsy was roused from her sleep by the smell of the kindling fired up in the wood-burning stove in the kitchen. But it was still nighttime. Her brother Doug—who, each morning, started the fire in the wood-burning stove so that their mother would have a hot stove on which to cook their breakfast oatmeal—would not be doing so in the dead of night.

The smell got stronger; now it reeked, heavy like soot. And for a moment, Patsy could only imagine that maybe she was asleep on the train, on the colored car. At the thought of being on that train, she sat up in bed. "Oh no, please no!" She felt around for her surroundings, and when her fingers touched the edge of the bed—sturdy with tall oak posts in each corner and framed with wide, carved panels at both the head and footboards and pressed up against the wall—she was comforted to know she was home. Eyes half-shut, yet drawn by the foul odor of soot, Patsy climbed over Laura and Jean to reach the floor. The girls did not stir. As she made her way to the door, her left foot got caught in the hem of her nightgown. She fell hard onto the kitchen floor, landing on her elbows.

"Aaycht!" Patsy let out a muffled cry. She rolled over onto her back and crossed both arms to rub her elbows. Cradling her arms, she raised her chin to tilt her head back and look around her: she was home, the room was empty, the stove was cold. But the smell was getting stronger. From where she lay, her head still tilted back, she could see out of the top of the kitchen window. And instead of the dark night sky, there was a red sky—a beautiful, bright-red sky. It was something she had never seen before.

Patsy scrambled up, elbows still throbbing, and ran around the kitchen table and pressed her face to the window. There she saw them:

gigantic red, orange, and yellow flames shooting up from the ground and reaching toward the sky. It was so bright and beautiful that she just stood there and stared—her gazed fixed on the powerful sight in front of her. Out of the corner of her eye, she thought she saw someone standing in the driveway. She could not be sure. Her eyes were set straight ahead, focused on the swirling, dancing colors. But she thought she saw Mr. Williams, Harold Williams from down the street, whom she had seen just the day before in the courtroom. Then the smell got stronger and the window felt hot. She backed away. She was at that instant fully awake. She looked and there was no man in the driveway.

Patsy looked at the red sky in front of her and finally knew what she saw. She screamed, "Daddy! Fire! Fire! The wood yard's on fire!"

It seemed that Douglas Ford was out of his bedroom and standing at the dining room window before Patsy could close her mouth.

"*Good God!*" her father yelled. "Fire! Fire in the wood yard! Everybody out of the house!"

May Ford came running out of the bedroom clutching Annie May to her chest. "Oh my

Lord," she cried. "Where are the girls? Douglas, get the girls!" To her son, asleep on his cot in the living room, she shouted, "Doug, baby, get up!"

Douglas was already coming back through the kitchen, Jean and Laura scooped up from bed, one under each arm. Doug Jr. jumped up from his bed and stumbled into the dining room to join the rest of the family.

"What? What's going on?" Doug asked.

Their father let the two girls down in the dining room. He looked at Doug and said anxiously, "Fire, son," he pointed to the window, "there's a fire in the wood yard."

The father looked around him. "Annie May, Patsy, Laura, Jean, Doug—OK, everybody's here," he said. "Now, out—everybody get over to the Yablonskis' house. Right now! Everybody out the front door!" their father yelled.

May, still holding Annie Mae, grabbed Jean's hand. "Patsy," their mother ordered, "you take Laura's hand. Come on children, you heard your father, let's go!"

Pointo started barking in the back yard.

Doug turned to his father. "What about Pointo? We've gotta get the dog!"

"The dog will be fine. He's behind the house, far enough away from the fire," their father said. Then he added brusquely, "Just get going, right now!"

May and the five children were out the door and on the front porch. Heavy smoke was in the air as they headed down the steps. They started to cough.

"Hold your head down," she said to her children, "and cover up your nose with your arm."

Patsy let go of Laura's hand. She stopped and turned and watched her father, still in the house, as he ran to the telephone. She heard him call the operator, saying, "Fire at 1950 Halleck Street! Yes, 1950 H-a-l-l-e-c-k. East of Dequindre. Send the fire truck! My wood yard's on fire! Yes. Yes." He slammed down the receiver.

"Patsy, get over here," her mother commanded. Patsy left the porch and ran next door.

May Ford was ringing the Yablonskis' doorbell and banging on the door. They stood there coughing. Someone answered the door. It was Mr. Yablonski.

"What is it? What is happening?" he asked sleepily as he opened the door. Then he saw the smoke.

"The wood yard's on fire!" May almost screamed.

"Oh my God!" he cried. "Yes! Come in, get the children inside!"

They all crowded into their neighbor's front room. Eva Yablonski entered the room, heard about the fire, and said, "Let me get blankets for the little ones. So they won't get the chill . . ."

May sat on the sofa, still holding Annie May in one arm with Jean leaning against the other.

"W-w-where's Vochu?" Jean asked when Mrs. Yablonski returned with an arm full of covers.

"She's asleep. She's a heavy sleeper. Nothing wakes her up, nothing," Mrs. Yablonski replied.

Doug, Patsy, and Laura stood and watched the commotion from the Yablonskis' front window. They saw neighbors gathering across the street. They watched the fire engine stop right at the Yablonskis' house, pulling in front of the hydrant. Their father stood on the sidewalk, a handkerchief up to his nose, talking to the firemen. He pointed and gestured while they connected the long hose to the hydrant.

Still looking out the window, Doug asked his mother, "We can't see what they're doing from here. Can we go out on the porch?"

"You can see enough right here. It's too dangerous out there. Too much smoke. You stay right here," their mother answered.

"Mama!" Patsy shrieked, turning to her mother.

"Goodness child, what's happened?" their mother asked, leaning forward and straining to see from the couch.

"My quilt! My quilt's in the summer kitchen! What if the summer kitchen catches on fire? What if my quilt burns, Mama?" Patsy said, almost in tears.

"Oh Patsy." Her mother settled back. "We can't do anything about that now. It'll be fine. And if not . . . if not, I'll help you start another one."

"No, Mama, you don't understand," she said. "Grandma said when I finish the quilt, I won't remember the colored car. I won't feel bad about

what happened when we had to get on that train
. . ." Patsy broke down in tears. "It has to be *that*
quilt. I have to get my quilt so I can finish it!"

Patsy fumbled with the doorknob and finally
swung open the front door. She ran down the
porch steps, through the firemen who were
carrying the hose past the Ford house. One of
the firemen yelled, "Get that child back! Get her
away from here!"

Patsy felt strong arms grab her across the
stomach. She twisted around and saw her father,
holding her against her will. "Good God, Patsy,
what are you doing out here?"

"My quilt," she explained, "my quilt is in the
summer kitchen! I've got to get my quilt!"

"Child, have you lost your senses? We can't
worry about that quilt right now . . ."

"But Daddy, you don't understand. Grandma
said that when I finish that quilt, I won't
remember the colored car and the bad things
about the train. She said all the bad feelings
will be gone. Please Daddy, I'm almost finished.
Don't let it burn—I've got to get that quilt."

While she talked, Douglas Ford was carrying
her up the steps of the Yablonskis' front porch.

May was standing there, holding the door open. "Patsy, Patsy, Patsy . . . if you were willing to run past a roaring fire to get to a piece of quilt, I don't think you'll be bothered anymore about that train and the colored car," her father said. He stepped into the living room and set her down. "Now stay put until the fire is out and it's safe for us to go home."

༈

When Patsy awoke, she, Doug, and Laura lay on the floor of their neighbors' living room, covered with blankets. Douglas Ford stood by the door, shaking his head as he talked to May and the Yablonskis.

"The fire chief said he smelled gasoline," Douglas said. "He thinks it was arson."

"Oh, my!" May said.

Mrs. Yablonski just shook her head.

Douglas turned to his wife. "Gather the children up, May. It's time to take them home."

He shook hands with their neighbors. "I can't thank you enough, both of you, for taking in my family like this. I won't forget it."

"We're neighbors, Mr. Ford," Mr. Yablonski

said. "We look after one another. That's what we do in the old country. That's what we do here."

༄

Douglas Ford led the way up the steps of the front porch. May Ford again carried Annie May and held Jean's hand. Patsy dragged along behind Doug and Laura. As their father unlocked the door, Doug asked, "Dad, can I go back behind the house and look after Pointo? Wanna make sure he's OK."

"He's fine. I looked after him," the father said. "But you can go on back. Be careful: it's wet and slippery by the side of the house. I'll let you in the back door."

Patsy stayed behind on the porch after the others had entered the house. Douglas held the door open. "Come on in, child. It's been a long night."

"Daddy? Did the summer kitchen burn?" she asked as they stepped into the living room.

"No. And I checked—your quilt is fine," her father answered.

Patsy smiled in relief.

"Daddy?"

Douglas closed the door and stood next to his daughter. "What is it, child?"

"Daddy, when I first saw the fire, I was looking out the kitchen window and . . ."

"Yes?"

"And, and I think I saw Mr. Williams in the driveway," she blurted out. Then she added quietly, "But I'm not sure if he was really there or not. Maybe I was dreaming. I'm not sure . . ."

Douglas Ford breathed in deeply and let out a long sigh. Then he said, "Maybe you saw him and maybe you didn't. All I known for sure, right now, is that the fire is out. And we're home, safe and sound."

He bent over and kissed her on the forehead. "Now go back to bed."

13

The Quilt

The summer kitchen did not burn, but the building had what Douglas Ford told his children was called smoke damage. In the week after the fire, Douglas and May Ford washed down everything in the front and back rooms of the summer kitchen. Douglas washed the walls and scrubbed the floors. May cleaned the soot off of all of her canning pots and utensils and wiped down her worktable. She mixed vinegar in with the laundry soap and washed the curtains, the sheets from the bed in the back room, and even Patsy's unfinished quilt. The vinegar—plus drying those things out in the hot sun on the clothesline—helped get out much of the smell. But sitting on the bench by the door as she completed the final step, putting the binding around the edge of her quilt, Patsy could still smell the ash and the soot in the wall behind her. A few times, when she leaned back and rested her head against the wall, the odor seemed almost as strong as on the night of the fire or, even more so, as strong as the smell of soot in the colored car.

Also in the week after the fire, one by one, the neighbor women returned to the summer kitchen.

"And you, Cleota, of all people!" Patsy heard her mother say as she chopped up the last of a bushel of firm bright-red tomatoes. Patsy sat on the edge of the bed in the back room putting the last stitches on her quilt while her sisters napped. She could see the two women as they talked. Mrs. Chambers answered, fanning herself with her apron, "I didn't think anything would come of it. I just signed my name to a piece of paper. And you know how sometimes late in the evening that saw—" She sounded out of breath as she talked.

"You should be ashamed of yourself," May said, pointing a finger at her that was dripping with tomato juice and cutting her off before she could finish the sentence.

Nothing more was said about it. And

Mrs. Chambers filled the buckets under the worktable with water before she left.

Later that evening, after dinner, Patsy asked her mother if Mrs. Chambers and Mrs. Carson and the other women who signed the petition were still her friends. May paused before she answered, "They're our neighbors. We have to live with them."

෴

The women—Mrs. Yablonski, Mrs. Chambers, and Mrs. Carson—stood by the worktable in the summer kitchen, held the finished quilt open between them, and admired Patsy's work. "My, my," Mrs. Chambers said. "Patsy, you do have a way with the needle." She looked over at May Ford. "She's gonna be sewing better than you if you don't watch out!" she said with a chuckle.

Her mother and the other women laughed along with Mrs. Chambers.

Patsy stood off a little to the side. "It would look better without that dirt from the train ride over on the side there," she said softly.

"Don't you worry about some little smudge like that," said Mrs. Yablonski.

"That's right, child," said Mrs. Carson. "And you covered most of it up with that nice binding you put around the edge. It hardly shows."

Mrs. Carson took the quilt edges from the other women, folded it up, and handed it to Patsy. "That'll look real nice on your bed," she said as Patsy laid it on the bench.

May looked over at Patsy. "Go in the house and get Laura," she said. "I want you girls to take some food over to Lena Williams." May then said to the women, "She's still having a really rough time of it, trying to feed that family . . ."

"What a shame it is," Mrs. Yablonski said, shaking her head.

Patsy stood there listening.

"Go on, now, and get your sister," her mother said.

When the two girls returned, May Ford had a row of jars lined up on the worktable filled with tomatoes, okra, string beans, peaches, grape jelly.

"This might be too much for you girls to carry," she said as she handed two jars to Laura.

"I guess I got carried away getting food from the cabinet."

Patsy brought her quilt over and spread it out on the table.

"Mama, put the rest of the jars here in the middle. Then we can fold it up like a sack," Patsy said.

"That's an idea," their mother said as she placed the jars in the quilt. "You still be careful walking so you don't trip and fall. You, too, Laura."

ം

The jars wrapped in the quilt knocked against each other as the sisters walked together. "I hope they don't crack. Maybe this wasn't such a good idea," Patsy said to Laura as they walked down Halleck Street.

A few more yards and the sisters had arrived at the Williamses' house. They walked around to the back door. There was no doorbell so Laura put down one of the jars she was carrying and knocked on the door. No one answered.

"Knock harder," Patsy said. Laura tried again.

Patsy saw a curtain open and a child's face

peeked out. She recognized Hazel, the older Williams girl. Then not too much later, the mother, Lena Williams, opened the door.

"Well, hello! Come on in, girls," Mrs. Williams said, leading them into the kitchen.

"My mother sent these jars over for you," Patsy said as Laura put her two jars down on the kitchen table and Patsy put down her sack and opened the quilt.

"Well, my, my, you tell your mother thank you kindly. She is just too kind!" Mrs. Williams said shaking her head. She looked at the two sisters and smiled. "I wish I had some peppermints or some kind of treat to give you girls to eat on your way home." She gestured around the kitchen with her hands open, as if giving the girls a tour. "But you can see, there's not much here."

There were no pots on the wood-burning stove, no smells of dinner cooking. Not even canisters holding flour and sugar on the kitchen counters or a bowl of fruit on the table.

"This food you've brought will really come in handy . . ." her voice trailed off. She looked down at the quilt. "Did your mother make this?" she asked.

"No, ma'am, I stitched it this summer. My grandmother taught me how to make a quilt when we went down to Tennessee for a visit."

"It's just lovely." There was a long silence as she looked down at the quilt and passed her hand over the fabric. "You girls'll be back in school next week, won't you?" she asked, raising her head and shifting her gaze over to Patsy and Laura.

The two girls nodded.

"I bet you girls are good at your lessons," Mrs. Williams said.

"Yes, ma'am," Patsy and Laura answered. "So, we'll be going now," Patsy said as she turned and started walking toward the back door. Laura followed.

"Well, all right now, like I said, you tell your mother thank you," Mrs. Williams said as the girls pushed open the door.

The sisters were out of the house and in the back yard when Mrs. Williams called after them, "Wait a minute! Here, baby," she said coming outside holding the quilt. "You left your quilt!"

Patsy turned to her. "No, it's for you, ma'am. I'm leaving it for you and your girls."

"Oh, child . . . ," Mrs. Williams said shaking her head. "It's been a long while since I had something of my own this nice," her voice breaking and tears welling up in her eyes. She walked over to Patsy and pulled her in close, giving her a long hug. "God bless you," she whispered.

⁓

May Ford looked up when the girls walked into the summer kitchen. She was wiping off the table. The pots were on the shelf. The room smelled like bleach.

"And how was Mrs. Williams?" May asked.

"She said thank you kindly for the food," Patsy answered.

May nodded and smiled.

"And Patsy let Mrs. Williams have her quilt!" Laura blurted out.

Patsy shot her a look.

"Well you did!" Laura said.

"What's this?" their mother asked, putting down her towel and looking straight at Patsy.

"She and the girls . . . they don't have much at all, Mama," Patsy said. "The kitchen was empty—I didn't see any food or anything. So, I don't know, I just left it there with her . . ."

"Patsy, my word, you're a good soul!"

"You know, Mama, as I was finishing the quilt, even when something reminded me of the colored car or that train ride, it didn't make me feel as sad as it used to. Now that I'm finished, I know Grandma was right—the bad feelings from that day . . ." Patsy put her hand up against her chest. "They're gone. I don't really feel them that much anymore."

Then Patsy added, "Anyway, I can make another quilt."

"That you can, dear, that you can," their mother said. "You can make many, many more."

Then, looking around the summer kitchen, their mother said, "Well, I guess that's enough for today. Patsy, go in the back room and get Jean and Annie May. Let's go in the house now. Your father will be home soon. You girls can help me start dinner."

Epilogue

The four Ford sisters all earned their bachelors and masters degrees and were educators in the Detroit Public Schools: Maber Ford Hill (Patsy) retired as an elementary school reading specialist; Marion Ford Thomas (Laura) retired as a high school science/mathematics department head; Jean Ford Fuqua (Jean) retired as an elementary school teacher and director of teacher interns for Wayne State University; and Gwili Ford Hanna (Annie May) retired as an elementary school science teacher and later pursued post-graduate studies in the health sciences. Their brother, Douglas Ford Jr., earned his medical degree and retired as a pediatrician.

Grandma Addie Jackson died on December 27, 1937. While she never saw her grandchildren again, the legacy of quilting continues as a tradition of the Ford family women to this day.

Epilogue

There were several more fires in the wood yard. No one was ever prosecuted.

About the Author

Jean Alicia Elster (BA, University of Michigan; JD, University of Detroit School of Law) is the author of *Who's Jim Hines?*—for ages 8 and older—published by Wayne State University Press (2008). *Who's Jim Hines?* was selected as one of the Library of Michigan's 2009 Michigan Notable Books. In addition, the Michigan Reading Association placed *Who's Jim Hines?* on the Great Lakes Great Books Award 2009–2010 ballot for grades 4–5. *Who's Jim Hines?* was also a *ForeWord* magazine 2008 Book of the Year Award Finalist in the category of Juvenile Fiction.

Elster is also the author of the children's book series Joe Joe in the City, which includes the books *Just Call Me Joe Joe* (2001), *I Have A Dream, Too!* (2002), *I'll Fly My Own Plane* (2002), and *I'll Do the Right Thing* (2003). She was awarded the 2002 Governors' Emerging Artist Award by ArtServe Michigan in recognition of the series, and in 2004, *I'll Do the Right Thing* received the *Atlanta Daily World* Choice Award in the category of children's books.

Elster has also edited several books, including *The Death Penalty*, *The Outbreak of the Civil War*, and *Building Up Zion's Walls: Ministry for Empowering the African American Family*. Her essays have appeared in many national publications, including *Ms.*, *World Vision*, *Black Child*, and *Christian Science Sentinel*. She also collaborated in the preparation of the manuscript for *Dear Mrs. Parks: A Dialogue with Today's Youth*, by Rosa Parks, which was honored with four awards, including the NAACP Image Award and the Teachers' Choice Award.

In recognition of outstanding work, Elster was awarded residencies at the internationally acclaimed Ragdale Foundation in Lake Forest, Illinois, in 2001, 2003, and 2005. She is frequently invited to speak at schools, libraries, and conferences throughout the state of Michigan and across the United States. In 2012, she was selected as the inaugural visiting author for The Lori Lutz Visiting Artist Series at The Roeper School in Bloomfield Hills, Michigan.

About the Author

She and her husband live in Detroit, Michigan. They are proud to acknowledge that their son is a journalist (BA) and their daughter is a school social worker (LLMSW).